D1580174

'My dance, I think.'

Without speaking, Dan took Stella's hand and pulled her against him, his eyes on hers as he glided backwards, taking her with him. It didn't surprise her that he was competent on the ice.

'I can't see why you're being so possessive.'

'Can't you?'

All the air seemed to have been sucked out of the atmosphere and suddenly she couldn't breathe. It was no longer about skating and Christmas; it was about her and Daniel.

'You're not making sense. In two days' time it's Christmas Eve. It's the two-year anniversary of the night you proposed to me—'

He inhaled sharply. 'I know what day it is.'

'And the day after that is Christmas Day.' Her cheeks stung from the cold. 'And that's the two-year anniversary of the night you broke off our engagement.'

'I know that, too. But I still don't find it easy watching you flirt with another man.'

Her fingers tightened on the hard muscle of his shoulders. 'Why would you even care?'

He spun her round, his mouth next to her ear. 'I care, Stella.' His voice was rough and male. 'You know I care.'

MISTLETOE & MATERNITY

Marriages made under the mistletoe

Snowflakes are starting to fall, Christmas carols are ringing out, and for the Buchannan brothers there are festive surprises in store…

These two gorgeous and dedicated doctors lost their faith in love a long time ago, but they're about to meet the women who can unlock their hearts and give them the most precious gift of all…

A family—just in time for Christmas!

Bestselling author Sarah Morgan brings you a brand-new duet full of all the magic of Christmas!

SNOWBOUND: MIRACLE MARRIAGE

and

CHRISTMAS EVE: DOORSTEP DELIVERY

Both available this month from Mills & Boon® Medical™ Romance

SNOWBOUND: MIRACLE MARRIAGE

BY
SARAH MORGAN

First published in Great Britain 2009
Large Print edition 2010
Harlequin Mills & Boon Limited,
Eton House, 18-24 Paradise Road,
Richmond, Surrey TW9 1SR

© Sarah Morgan 2009

ISBN: 978 0 263 21089 7

Printed and bound in Great Britain
by CPI Antony Rowe, Chippenham, Wiltshire

Sarah Morgan is a British writer who regularly tops the bestseller lists with her lively stories for both Mills & Boon® Medical™ and Modern™.

As a child Sarah dreamed of being a writer, and although she took a few interesting detours on the way she is now living that dream. She firmly believes that reading romance is one of the most satisfying and fat-free escapist pleasures available. Her stories are unashamedly optimistic, and she is always pleased when she receives letters from readers saying that her books have helped them through hard times.

RT Book Reviews has described her writing as 'action-packed and sexy'.

Sarah lives near London with her husband and two children, who innocently provide an endless supply of authentic dialogue. When she isn't writing or nagging about homework Sarah enjoys music, movies, and any activity that takes her outdoors.

Recent titles by the same author:

Medical™ Romance
THE GREEK BILLIONAIRE'S LOVE-CHILD
ITALIAN DOCTOR, SLEIGH-BELL BRIDE
THE REBEL DOCTOR'S BRIDE**
THE ITALIAN'S NEW-YEAR MARRIAGE WISH*

*Brides of Penhally Bay
**Glenmore Island Doctors

Sarah Morgan also writes for Modern™ Romance. Her sexy heroes and feisty heroines aren't to be missed!

Modern™ Romance
POWERFUL GREEK, UNWORLDLY WIFE
CAPELLI'S CAPTIVE VIRGIN
THE PRINCE'S WAITRESS WIFE

To Lucy, whose happy smile
and cheerful nature
never fail to brighten my day

PROLOGUE

'I'M OVER him. Really. That's why I'm back.' Stella stamped the snow from her boots and levered them off on the doorstep of the converted stable. 'Two years is a long time. Long enough to gain some perspective on things.' She glanced at the man next to her and caught her breath because he was so like his brother. And yet so different. *This man hadn't smashed her dreams into a million tiny pieces.* 'Are you sure it's a good idea for me to live in your stable?'

'It's nearly Christmas,' he drawled, a gleam of humour in his eyes as he stood aside to let her pass. 'A stable is prime accommodation, haven't you heard?'

Stella smiled, but beneath the smile was a shiver of trepidation.

Christmas.

Once, it had been her favourite time of year.

But that had been before every glittering silver bauble reminded her of the engagement ring she'd worn for such a short space of time.

Putting her life back together had taken time, effort and determination. And she was about to test just how far she'd come.

She'd kept her emotions safely boxed away, like Christmas decorations that were no longer needed. What if the box suddenly opened, spilling all those emotions back into her life?

For a terrifying moment it felt as though two years of healing was about to be undone and Stella stepped quickly inside her new home, hiding her feelings from the man watching her. He was a doctor as well as a friend. She knew how much he saw.

Her feet sank into the soft, cream rug that covered much of the pale wooden floor and she blinked rapidly to clear the tears, angry with herself. *No more tears,* wasn't that what she'd promised herself? 'I suspect this is a little more comfortable than the original stable. You've performed miracles, Patrick. When I last saw this two years ago, it still had a horse in it.' She was making polite conversation but it was impossible to ignore the gnawing anxiety in her stomach.

'Stella, will you drop the act?' He slammed the door shut on the snow and the freezing December air. 'You're a nervous wreck. Pale. Jumpy. Looking over your shoulder in case Daniel suddenly turns up. He isn't going to. He's up to his elbows in blood and drama at the hospital. It's just you and me. We drowned our sorrows together two years ago. If you can't be honest with me, who can you be honest with?'

Stella tugged off her gloves. 'He's your brother. That makes it awkward.'

'The fact that he's my brother doesn't blind me to his faults.' Patrick dropped the keys on the table. 'Neither does it affect our friendship. We kept each other going over that nightmare Christmas. Don't think I've forgotten that.'

Stella felt her insides wobble and wondered whether it was a mistake to pursue this conversation. In a way it had been easier living and working among people who didn't know— people who weren't watching to see how she was coping. 'I'm nervous about seeing him,' she said finally. 'Of course I am.'

'I'm not surprised. Stella, you were engaged.'

'For about five minutes.' She walked towards the wood-burning stove and stared at the glass. 'I just wish he hadn't broken it off at Christmas. It made it harder, somehow.'

'He shouldn't have broken it off at all.'

'That was inevitable.' She turned, resigned to having the conversation she'd hoped to avoid. 'Daniel doesn't believe he'd be a good husband and he definitely doesn't think he'd be a good father—you know how his mind works. The surprise wasn't that he broke off the engagement, but that he proposed to me in the first place. If I'd been stronger, I would have said no. I knew it wasn't what he wanted.' Lost in thought, dwelling in the land of 'what if', Stella lifted one of the logs piled in a basket, ready to be used on the fire, and rubbed her fingers along the rough bark. Then she looked at Patrick. 'Enough of me. How are *you* doing? If anything, that Christmas was worse for you than it was for me. Your wife left.'

'The difference is that Carly and I weren't in love. I was angry with her for ending it at Christmas, and I feel for the children not having a mother around, but for myself…' He gave a dismissive shrug. 'The one thing about being unhappily married is that divorce feels like a blessing. But I'm aware that I'm probably part of the reason that Daniel got cold feet.'

'I think it was more like frostbite than cold feet,' Stella said lightly, 'and it wasn't your fault.'

'Carly walked out on Christmas Eve. Daniel broke off your engagement on the same day. Believe me, there was a connection.'

Remembering just how awful that Christmas had been for both of them, Stella sighed. 'You and I spent it on our own, trying to smile around your kids, do you remember?'

'I remember that you were brave,' Patrick said gruffly, reaching out and squeezing her shoulder. 'After Daniel walked out, you disappeared for five minutes and then came back with your make-up on and a smile on your face, determined to give my children a good time. Because of you, I don't think Alfie even noticed that his mother wasn't there.'

'The children gave me something to focus on. And you and I *did* share that bottle of champagne, which helped. And we ate every scrap of chocolate from the Christmas tree.'

'Then I went and picked up a kitten from the farmer next door, do you remember?'

It was one of the few happy memories among the miserable ones. 'Giving Alfie that kitten was an inspired idea. And it was *gorgeous*.'

'That kitten is now a cat and has just produced kittens of her own.'

'Really? Alfie must love that.'

'I've said he can keep two. I have to find homes for the other two. Our life is chaotic enough without four kittens.' Patrick's gaze settled on her face. 'You really were brave, Stella. I know how much you love Dan. The fact that you held it together was nothing short of amazing.'

'If you'd seen me two weeks later, you wouldn't have thought I was amazing. I was in pieces.'

'I'm not surprised.'

Talking about the past had removed any awkwardness between them. 'I'm worried about how Daniel is going to react when he finds out that I'm living in your stable.'

'I don't care what he thinks.' Tough, calm and sure of himself, Patrick removed the log from her hands. 'My property. My decision.'

"Well, that's a non-confrontational approach.'

Stella watched as he opened the wood-burning stove. 'I don't want to cause a problem between you. I don't want you falling out over me.'

'We have to fall out over something. It won't be the first time it's a woman. I still owe him for stealing Nancy Potter away from me when I was eight. I adored that girl. I've had a thing for pigtails ever since.' His smile was slow and sexy and Stella wondered for the millionth time why she couldn't have fallen for him instead of his brother.

You always have to do things the hard way, Stella.

Dismissing her mother's voice from her head, Stella slid her hands into the back pockets of her jeans and forced herself to keep it light. 'So— was this Nancy Potter pretty?'

'She had red hair and a fierce temper.'

'Sounds scary.'

'Relationships are always scary.'

She wasn't going to argue with that. 'You and I both want the same out of life. I met you and Dan at exactly the same time, that week I started at the hospital five years ago. Why couldn't you and I have fallen in love with each other?'

Patrick fed the log into the stove. 'Because you're a beautiful blonde and I hate stereotypes.'

Stella lifted a hand to her hair. 'I could dye it black?'

'Wouldn't make any difference. There was never any chemistry between us.'

Stella watched his muscles flex as he reached for another log. 'Do you remember that time you kissed me, just to check?'

'Daniel punched me immediately afterwards.' Patrick lit the fire. 'He didn't want you involved with me in case I hurt you.'

They exchanged a look, both thinking the same thing.

That, in the end, it had been Daniel who had hurt her.

'Am I going to be able to do this?' Stella was asking herself as much as him. 'Am I going to be able to work alongside him every day and not wish I was with him?'

'You tell me. Are you?'

Stella gave a murmur of frustration. 'I don't know. I hope so.' She paced the length of the living room, hating herself for being so unsure and indecisive. 'Yes, of course I can do it. And if it feels difficult—well, I just need to keep reminding myself that he and I don't want the same things out of life.'

Patrick coaxed the flame to life. 'You just need to keep reminding yourself that when it comes to women, Daniel is nothing but trouble. We Buchannans are *seriously* bad at relationships.'

'*You're* not.'

He rocked back on his heels. 'I'm divorced, Stella.'

'Your wife was clearly deranged.'

'Or maybe I'm not easy to live with.'

'No man is easy to live with,' Stella said dryly. 'You're a different species. I just wish I'd listened to you when you warned me about Dan.'

'It wouldn't have made a difference. Women never listen when it comes to Daniel. It's those blue eyes of his. For some reason I've never understood, he can seduce a woman with a single glance.' Patrick stood up and brushed the dust from his long black coat. 'I admire you. He wouldn't give you marriage so you walked away. You refused to accept less than you deserve.'

Stella watched as the fire whispered and licked

at the logs and then flared to life. 'Why does that sound better than it feels?'

'Because the right thing isn't always the easy thing.' Patrick studied her for a long moment. 'Why now? Why did you come back now?'

As the room grew warmer, Stella unwound the scarf from her neck. 'Because I hated London. Because two years is a long time. Because I worked here for three years and I miss all my friends. Because I can see how wrong Daniel was for me. And because I really am over him.' *Dear God, please let her be over him...*

Patrick gave her a long, hard look. 'If you're over him, why haven't you told him you're back?'

Stella felt her heart lurch and she glanced from the stove to the exposed beams. 'How did you find time to do this up?'

'I didn't. I just wrote cheques. And stop changing the subject.'

'Why would I tell him I'm back? We haven't had any contact since that nightmare Christmas two years ago. Not once.' *They'd been so close, and yet he hadn't even contacted her to see how she was.* 'He doesn't know I'm planning to live with his brother. He doesn't know I've got a job in the emergency department. If I rang him and said I was coming back he might think I was dropping hints. Hoping to get back together or something. That would be awkward and embarrassing.'

'So, instead, you're going to walk into the emergency department tomorrow and surprise him.' Patrick gave a sardonic smile. 'I hate to disillusion you, angel, but I don't think that approach is going to steer you away from awkward and embarrassing.'

'Maybe not, but there won't be an opportunity for conversation. There's no time to talk about personal stuff in the emergency department, especially not at Christmas when it's so busy.' Stella flopped down on the comfortable sofa. 'And one of the advantages of having been engaged for less than twenty-four hours is that most people didn't know about it.'

Patrick spread his hands in a gesture of apology. 'What can I say? Dan's always shied away from commitment. Our parents' marriage was ugly, you know that. *Really* ugly. Not an example anyone in their right mind would be in a hurry to follow.'

'It didn't stop you marrying.'

'Maybe it should have done.' His tone weary, Patrick walked to the window. 'I suppose I wanted to create something I'd never had—I wanted the whole family thing. Dan just rejected it. And maybe he was the sensible one given that my ex-wife is now living in New York and my children no longer have a mother.'

'I'm sorry about your divorce,' Stella said softly, watching as Patrick's broad shoulders tensed.

'Don't be sorry for me. I'm fine. It's just the kids I worry about.'

'I'm dying to see them. They won't remember me.'

'Alfie remembers you.' Patrick turned with a smile. 'He was eight when you left and you've been sending him thoughtful birthday presents. He's dying to show you our kittens. And you won't recognise Posy, she's grown so much.'

'I can't believe she's three.'

'She's very mischievous. Generally creating havoc.'

'And what about you? Any women in your life?'

'Thousands,' Patrick drawled, a wicked gleam in his blue eyes. 'I find I can't get through the day without stripping at least one midwife naked.'

'You can joke, but I happen to know that ninety-five per cent of the midwives in your department would be only too happy to be stripped naked by you.'

'What am I doing wrong with the other five per cent?'

'He's a man.'

'Ah.' Laughing, he tilted his head. 'Your turn to tell all. Did you find yourself a decent rebound relationship to cure you of my brother?'

Stella straightened her shoulders. 'Not yet, but I'm working on it. It's my Christmas present to myself. A love life. I've made a list.'

'A list of men?'

'No!' Stella laughed. 'A list of qualities. You know—things I won't compromise on.'

'Like tall, dark, handsome, rich...' Realising what he'd said, Patrick threw her an apologetic look but Stella managed a smile.

'That sounds too much like Dan,' she said lightly. 'I was thinking more of must want marriage and children.' She glanced around her. 'Does this place have an internet connection?'

'High-speed broadband—why?'

'Because I've joined an internet dating agency.

I've decided that this time I'm going to be more analytical about the whole thing. It was crazy, falling for Daniel. He had "unsuitable" stamped on his forehead. If I'd made him fill out a questionnaire he never would have passed "go". This time I'm weeding out all the men who aren't right for me. I posted a description of myself last month and I've had three hundred and fifty replies.'

'You're going to be busy.'

'Maybe you should do the same thing?'

'I don't have time to date. Between the children, the kittens and the hospital, I'm lucky if I sleep. And, anyway, I wouldn't expose the kids to another woman. Too complicated. Talking of which, I'd better get going. The labour ward rang half an hour ago to warn me they have a woman who isn't progressing as she should be. I need to check her out.' Patrick scooped the keys from the table and handed them to her. 'These are for you. You're my first tenant so if there's anything I need to know about the place, just tell me. They're forecasting constant snow between now and Christmas so if the heating isn't high enough, light the fire or adjust the thermostat.'

'I'll light the fire. It's so cosy. And if you need

any babysitting, I'm right here. It's so good to be home. I've been away too long.'

'I hope you don't find it isolated after city life. If you're internet dating, surely you're more likely to find Mr Right in London?'

'I don't think so.' Stella stared at the craggy outline of the mountains in the distance. 'This place is in my blood. I need a man who understands that. A man who loves it as much as I do.'

'Well, I wish you luck.' Patrick strolled towards the door and Stella turned to look at him.

'Just one thing…' Her heart pounding, she tried to sound casual. 'Is Daniel seeing anyone?'

Patrick paused with his hand on the doorhandle. 'Are you sure you want me to answer that question?'

'Yes.' Stella licked her lips. 'I'd rather hear it from you. It will be easier if I'm prepared.'

'He *is* seeing someone.' Patrick's voice was gentle and his eyes held hers. 'She's a lawyer. Career-woman. Workaholic. About as maternal as a cactus.'

'Oh. OK.' Feeling suddenly cold, Stella rubbed her hands over her arms. Because Patrick was watching her intently, she smiled. 'She sounds perfect for him. Not the sort to want marriage and a family. That's good. Great. Really, I mean it. I—I'm glad he's happy.'

Patrick studied her face for a long time and then he opened the door, letting in a blast of ice-cold air. 'I said he was seeing someone. I said she reminded me of a cactus. I never said that he was happy.'

And, with that cryptic comment and an enigmatic smile, he closed the door behind him.

CHAPTER ONE

'THE mountain rescue team are bringing in a boy who slipped on a school adventure trip. It was a very tricky rescue, by all accounts. He was wedged in a steep gully, too badly injured to move. And the weather was too bad for the helicopter to winch him out.' Ellie, the emergency department sister, checked the notes she'd made. 'Nasty compound fracture of the tibial shaft. I'm guessing that the poor boy had more adventure than he was planning for.'

'Oh, the poor thing!' Stella felt a stab of sympathy. 'So how did they get him out?'

'One of the team abseiled down into the gully. Sat in the freezing cold with him and figured out a way to achieve the impossible,' Ellie said dryly. 'Heroic rescue by all accounts. I was hoping you'd take this one for me. It might be a bit complicated and you were always good with complicated. It's so good to have you back. I missed you. Did they teach you anything new in that fancy hospital in London?'

'Only how to deal with stabbings and gunshot wounds, which isn't a lot of use up here in Cumbria. I missed you, too, and I can't wait to catch up properly.' Her friendship with Ellie was another reason she'd come back. 'We ought to go out. Pizza? Movie?'

'Both!' Ellie hugged her. 'But it will have to be early. I have to be in bed by nine or I can't function. The kids are exhausting at the moment.'

Stella felt a sudden stab of envy. 'I can't wait to see them. Are they looking forward to Christmas?'

'Are you joking? They're so over-excited they can't sleep and there's still another three weeks to go. Ben and I will be frayed by Christmas Eve.'

But frayed in a good way, Stella thought wistfully, longing for the chance to be similarly frayed. She wouldn't *want* to sleep if she had a baby. She'd just want to lie awake all night, staring in wonder.

'I'll go and prepare Resus.' Knowing that it was stupid to dwell on what she didn't have, Stella walked with Ellie towards the resuscitation room. 'So which one of the team performed the daring rescue? Was it your Ben?'

'No.' Ellie pushed open the doors to Resus. 'It was your Dan.'

Stella stopped, feeling as though her heart had been left two metres behind her body. 'Daniel?'

'Yes. He's bringing the boy in now.' Ellie peered at her face. 'I think you've just answered my next question, which was going to be, "Are you still in love with him?"'

'I'm not in love with him.'

'This is me you're talking to.'

'I'm not in love with him.'

'All right, we'll argue about that some other time. For now what I need to know is whether you can work with him.'

Stella was grateful for the acting classes she'd taken as a child. They helped her pull her features into an expression that said 'unconcerned'.

In less than five minutes she was going to see him. This was the moment she'd been dreading. The whole thing felt like some sort of test. How far had she come? Had she recovered enough to be able to look at Daniel and not want him? Aware that some sort of response was required, she nodded. 'I can work with him. He's a very talented doctor.' She consoled herself with the fact that at least the second half of that sentence wasn't a lie. 'Why would it be a problem?'

Ellie sighed and then gave her a quick hug. 'Stella, this is a big thing for you, I know. I watched you fall in love with Dan. I know what he meant to you.'

'And you watched when it fell apart.'

'You were engaged.'

'For about five minutes. Two years ago. *Big* mistake. I don't intend to repeat it. Dan and I are history.' Stella pulled away from her. 'And I have a date tomorrow. He calls himself "Caring of Cumbria". Blond, sensitive, loves romantic nights in by the fire and is looking for a long-term relationship with the right woman.'

Ellie laughed. 'Sounds the complete opposite of Dangerous Dan.'

'Who is dark, *in*sensitive, likes hot sex by the fire and short-term relationships with the wrong women. You see? If I'd analysed him properly I would have run a mile.' Gaining confidence from that thought, Stella walked across the room. 'All right, what am I likely to need?'

'Do you want me to hang around?'

'In case we kill each other?' Stella pulled on an apron and a pair of gloves. 'I hope we'll be more civilised than that. Is there anything else I should know about the patient?'

'Dan will tell you when he gets here. He's going to deal with it himself.' With that unsettling announcement, Ellie hurried out of the room and seconds later the door swung open again.

The man guiding the stretcher into the room was tall and powerfully built, his outdoor clothing adding bulk to his muscular shoulders. 'All right, Sam.' His voice was calm and confident as he talked to the boy. 'Now I've got some proper equipment, I can make you a bit more comfortable.' He turned to the two junior doctors who were flanking him. 'I put a line in at the scene, but I want you to get another one in straight away. He's had morphine and the leg is splinted. I need another bag of fluid and…' Daniel glanced up, saw Stella and lost his thread.

Their relationship had begun with a single look, *a single look that had altered the future for both of them.*

Non-verbal communication had been their speciality—a knowing glance, a touch, a smile that was more of a promise—and if she'd hoped that the damage that lay behind them would have changed anything, she was disappointed.

The sudden jolt of chemistry was powerful enough to have Stella reaching out to hold the side of the trolley. It was as if she'd touched a high-voltage cable and a thousand memories shot through her, all of them including a man with ice-blue eyes and a dangerously sexy smile.

But the smile wasn't in evidence today.

His lean, handsome face was serious, his expression doing nothing to soften the hardness of the man.

It was unfortunate that he'd come straight from a rescue, Stella thought weakly. Stubble suited him. The first thing she'd done every morning had been to drag her fingers over the darkness of his jaw, just before she'd kissed him…

Her stomach took a dive. 'Hello, Daniel.'

He unzipped the neck of his jacket roughly, as if it was choking him. 'Stella?' His voice was hoarse and shocked and suddenly she couldn't breathe because the memories were out of control.

His breath hot on her neck; his skilled,

knowing hands on her trembling body; that same husky voice murmuring her name.

She gazed back at him, the only man who'd ever had this effect on her.

In London she'd hoped to meet someone who would make her forget Daniel. But how did you forget a face as absurdly handsome as his? How did you forget six feet two of arrogant masculinity? Who, out of the many doctors she'd met during her period of self-imposed exile, would have been capable of abseiling into a narrow ravine and masterminding the rescue of a severely injured boy?

Who would have had the ability to make her care so much that when it had ended, part of her had ceased to function?

Remembering the agony was what saved her. Stella turned back to the patient, reminding herself that 'Caring of Cumbria' liked long walks and was looking for commitment. 'Hello, Sam.' She walked over to the stretcher and smiled at the white-faced boy. 'I hear you've had a bit of an exciting day.'

He looked impossibly young and he turned his head to look at Daniel, fear and hero-worship mingling in his eyes. 'You promised you wouldn't leave me. You said—'

'I know what I said.' Daniel's voice was rough and he curved his hand over the boy's shoulder. 'And I'm not leaving you. But I do need to try and sort out that leg of yours. Trust me. Just do as I say and you're going to be all right.'

Always In control. Always in charge.

Trust me.

Stella gritted her teeth. *Trust me to break your heart.* But she noticed that his hand stayed on the boy's shoulder, providing the contact and reassurance that was so obviously needed as he gave the other doctors a series of instructions.

She guided the stretcher alongside the trolley. 'We're just going to move you across, Sam.'

'You're working here?' Daniel's harsh interruption made her flinch and Stella gently removed the blanket covering the boy.

Wasn't it obvious? 'I've called the radiologist.'

'Wait.' His hand covered hers, stopping her. 'We move him on my count, not before.'

She'd forgotten what it was like, working with him. When he was in Resus, he was the one in command. Which was why this particular hospital had such impressive success rates, she thought dryly. Her heart thumping, Stella glanced down at the strength of his fingers covering hers and gently eased her hand away. 'Fine. On your count.'

Registering her withdrawal, his jaw tensed and his eyes narrowed dangerously. 'Why did no one tell me you were back?'

'Because the medical staff aren't usually interested in nursing appointments,' Stella said calmly, wondering if he was even aware that the other medical staff in the room were watching them, wondering what was going on.

Nothing was going on, she told herself firmly. *Nothing, except an awkward first meeting.*

They transferred the boy from stretcher to trolley, and Daniel gave Stella a fulminating look that warned her that the conversation was far from over. Then he turned back to the frightened child and proceeded to demonstrate how he'd earned his reputation as a ferociously talented emergency doctor.

Maintaining a casual flow of conversation that distracted the boy, he examined him thoroughly, his skilled hands looking for injuries he hadn't already identified

'How's that pain, Sam?'

'It's OK.' But the boy's face was grey and Daniel glanced towards one of his colleagues.

'Is that line in yet?'

'Just about to do that now.' The more junior doctor was obviously keen to ask questions. 'So what's the Gustilo classification? Was there extensive tissue loss? Much bone exposure? This is an orthopaedic emergency, right?' His tactless observation drew a terrified sound from the boy and he clutched Daniel's arm.

'I feel sick.'

Panic, Stella thought to herself and Daniel gave him a warm smile.

'You're doing fine, Sam. I'm not worried and if I'm not worried, you don't need to be worried.' He glanced towards the doctor who had spoken and Stella saw his eyes narrow dangerously. 'Get that line in,' he murmured softly, 'and I'll talk to you about the case later.'

And about other things, Stella thought to herself. Daniel Buchannan was too much of a perfectionist to allow the younger doctor's slip to pass without comment.

'Just breathe for me, Sam,' she said softly. 'I'm

going to attach these wires to you so that we can monitor your pulse and blood pressure without having to disturb you.'

The boy looked at her gratefully. 'You probably think I'm a baby.'

'Babies don't climb in Devil's Gully.' Stella wrapped the blood-pressure cuff around his arm. 'I've seen it from the top. Never had the nerve to go down.'

Sam closed his eyes. 'My mum is going to kill me.'

'She'll just be glad you're all right.' Stella looked at the monitor, noticing the rapid pulse rate and the low blood pressure. She looked at Daniel and he inclined his head briefly, but said nothing that would worry the boy.

'I'm going to give you something else for the pain and sickness in just a moment, Sam,' he said gently, checking the boy's abdomen. 'Stella, I want to do a FAST scan. There might be some bleeding here.'

Stella reached for the machine, still talking to the boy. 'I can't believe you climbed that bit of the mountain,' she said briskly, reaching for the drugs that Daniel was going to need. 'It's a tricky route, even in summer. Steep.' She talked as she worked, keeping the boy's attention.

'It was snowy and I went too close to the edge.'

Picturing the scene, Stella suppressed a shudder. The boy had been lucky to escape with his life. Knowing the harsh, unforgiving terrain, she also knew that Daniel must have risked his own life to save the child. 'That story is going to get you lots of sympathy over Christmas,' she said lightly. 'And bigger presents.'

The child's face brightened slightly. 'Do you think so?'

'I'm sure.' Stella grinned and put the syringes on a tray. 'Start planning your Christmas list now.'

The boy managed a smile and then groaned as a spasm of pain took hold. The groan turned to a sob and he looked at Daniel, his eyes terrified. 'Am I going to die? I feel sick. And dizzy. Like everything is far away.'

When he needed reassurance, he looked at Daniel, Stella noticed. He'd bonded with the man who had saved his life.

'You're not going to die.' Daniel spoke firmly, his hand still on the boy's shoulder. 'If patients die, I get fired. And I need the money.'

The sound the boy made was halfway between laughter and a sob. 'To run that fancy sports car you told me about?'

'Yeah—that and other things.'

'Women?'

Daniel's eyes gleamed. 'They're expensive things, women.' Without moving his eyes from the patient, he held out his hand and Stella slipped the syringe into it, knowing exactly what he wanted.

'Morphine and cyclizine.'

'I know my leg is a mess,' Sam murmured, still looking at Daniel. 'I saw it before you put the splint on. It looked disgusting. And that other doctor said it was a medical emergency.'

'It's nothing we can't deal with,' Daniel said smoothly, checking the drug before administering it. 'Take no notice of my colleague. We doctors love drama—makes us feel powerful and important. Don't you watch the TV? It's how we pull the girls. There's a pretty nurse in the room. He's trying to impress her.'

The boy gave a weak grin. 'Those medical dramas mostly make me feel sick.'

'Me, too,' Daniel said blithely, dropping the empty syringe back onto the tray. 'Probably why

I'm still single. I haven't got what it takes to pull the girls. All right, Sam, this is what we're going to do. I've just given you another dose of medicine for pain and sickness because I can see that's starting to bother you again. And now my friend here is going to put another needle in your vein.'

The boy's eyes closed. 'I still feel sick.'

'That will pass in a minute,' Daniel murmured, his gaze flickering to the monitor that displayed the boy's pulse and blood pressure. 'I'm right here, Sam. Don't you worry. Everything is going to be fine. In three weeks' time, you're going to be eating your turkey and opening those presents.'

How could he possibly think he wouldn't make a good father? Stella wondered numbly. For a man who claimed to know nothing about children, he was astonishingly empathetic.

Sam obviously agreed because he never took his eyes from Daniel's face. 'I'll never forget you climbing down that slippery bit,' the boy mumbled. 'You deserve a medal or something.'

Daniel grinned, moving to one side while the radiologist prepared to take the X-rays. 'Unfortunately I never get what I deserve. What was your reward supposed to be for battling through the snow and wind?'

'My adventure badge. But I don't suppose I'll get it now because I didn't finish the trip.' The boy moaned as the radiologist moved his leg slightly. 'I wish I'd never signed up for it.'

'You were unlucky, that's all. When you're recovered give me a call and I'll take you up there. The views are fantastic from the top. You'll get your adventure badge—I'm sure about that.' Daniel was working, examining the boy properly and murmuring instructions in a voice so calm that the boy remained unaware of the seriousness of his injuries. 'Stella, how are the distal pulses?'

'Strong.' Stella checked that the blood supply to the lower limb was satisfactory while the casualty officer secured the second line and took the bloods that Daniel had ordered.

'Do you want me to uncover the wound and take a photograph?'

'I did that at the scene. I don't want the dressing removed. The next time that wound is being exposed to air is in the operating theatre. Camera in my left pocket.' Daniel turned slightly so that Stella could retrieve it and she tensed as she plunged her hand into his pocket.

His eyes met hers for a moment and she backed away, her fingers clutching the camera.

'Antibiotics and tetanus,' Daniel said roughly, and Stella turned away to prepare the drugs, knowing that her face was pink.

This was turning out to be much, much harder than she'd anticipated.

Was this going to get easier with time?

She certainly hoped so.

It wasn't the working together that was the problem—that was as smooth as ever. It was the emotion behind it. It was impossible to switch off.

'Daniel?' Ellie put her head round the door, her face worried. 'I know you're not officially on duty but we're having a nightmare out here. I suppose it's the snow and ice—the roads are lethal. I've got a pregnant woman coming in. She and her husband were involved in a car accident. Might you be able to—?'

'Yes. As long as she doesn't mind being seen by a doctor in full outdoor gear.' Daniel injected the antibiotic into the cannula, his eyes on his patient's face. 'I've been in the mountains for eight hours.

At some point I need to get back to base, drop the equipment and debrief. Where is everyone else? What's the ETA of your pregnant woman?'

'Ambulance Control just phoned. She's about eight minutes away.'

'That should give me time to get Sam down to Theatre. Give me a shout when she arrives.' Daniel glanced at Stella. 'Any sign of the orthopaedic guys?'

'We're here.' A slim man with sandy-coloured hair hurried into the room. 'Sorry. Black ice has kept us busy. I've only just got out of Theatre.' He looked at Daniel's bulky outdoor gear. 'Is this a new uniform for the emergency department?'

'Daniel?' The boy's hand shot out and clutched Daniel's arm again. There was fear in his eyes. 'Are they going to put me to sleep? Will I feel anything? Did you get hold of my mum?'

'They are going to put you to sleep and, no, you won't feel anything.' Daniel's voice was soft. 'I spoke to your mum. She's on her way.'

'Will you stay with me until she gets here?'

A muscle worked in Daniel's dark jaw. 'Are you kidding? You're wearing half my equipment— and it's the expensive half. There's no way I'm letting you out of my sight. We're going to take you straight to Theatre and get that leg of yours stuck back together in time for Christmas.' His glaze flickered to his colleague. 'Are you ready?'

'You're coming, too?' The man looked startled but Daniel's gaze was cool.

'I'll stay with him until he's under.'

The orthopaedic surgeon picked up the charts and gave a brief nod. 'All right. Well, you're obviously needed back here, so let's move.'

'If my pregnant patient was eight minutes away three minutes ago then I have five minutes.' Daniel glanced at his watch. 'I'll be back in five minutes.'

He'd been out on an exposed mountainside for eight hours and he had five minutes in which he could have grabbed a hot drink. Instead he was going to accompany a frightened child to the anaesthetic room.

Stella gritted her teeth. All the reasons why she'd fallen in love with Daniel in the first place were still there. Nothing had changed.

'Go.' She started clearing Resus. 'I'll sort things out here.'

She barely had time to run through another bag of fluid and restock, before the paramedics arrived with the pregnant woman. After listening to the handover by the paramedics, Stella tried to make her patient more comfortable.

Her face was bleeding slightly from several small lacerations and a livid bruise was already forming over one cheekbone. 'I'm so worried about the baby. We've been trying for five years—' Her voice broke and she rubbed her hand over her swollen abdomen. 'If anything happens to him I'll—'

'We're going to check you *and* the baby, Fiona,' Stella soothed, glancing towards the door as Daniel strode in. 'This is Dr Buchannan, one of our consultants.'

Fiona looked in astonishment at Daniel's outdoor clothing and he shrugged.

'It's cold in this department,' he drawled, and she gave a choked laugh.

'I read an article about you last summer. You're one of three doctors in the emergency department that volunteer for the mountain rescue team.'

'That's right.' Daniel glanced at the monitor that Stella had connected to the patient, tracking the readings. 'There's Sean Nicholson, although we do keep telling him he's getting a bit too old for tramping up in the hills. And there's Ben— both of whom are treating other patients, which is why you have me. Technically I'm off duty but there's no rest for the wicked. I see Stella's already given you oxygen.' He turned to Stella. 'I'd forgotten what it's like to work with a nurse who is always one step ahead of me.'

Stella's hands trembled slightly as she attached Fiona to the CTG machine. 'This will help us get a feel for how your baby is doing.' She adjusted the elastic until she was satisfied with the reading. 'Daniel—do you want me to call Obstetrics and get someone down here?'

'I'll take a look at her first. Monitors only tell you so much—I learned that lesson as a medical student when the monitor told me a woman wasn't having contractions. She delivered the baby five minutes later. I was more shocked than she was.' Daniel took off his jacket, washed his hands and pulled on a pair of gloves. 'Have you had any problems in the pregnancy, Fiona? Anything you think I should know about?'

If sexual attraction was enough to hold two people together then they would have stuck like glue, Stella thought helplessly, watching the flex of his biceps as he worked.

'It's all been really easy.' Fiona twisted her wedding ring round her finger. 'I've been doing everything by the book. It's our first baby. And I'm terrified.' Her voice wobbled. 'Do you have kids?'

Stella's gaze met Daniel's briefly.

'No.' There was a sudden coolness to his tone. 'I don't.'

'It changes you,' Fiona said simply. 'All I care about is this baby. I suppose that's part of being a mother.'

Daniel didn't respond and Stella stayed silent, too.

Marriage, motherhood, maternity—Daniel's three least favourite topics of conversation. And she should know. They'd had that conversation on numerous memorable occasions. *Memorable for all the wrong reasons.*

'It's natural to be concerned about the baby.' Daniel spoke the words the woman needed to hear, but Stella sensed that part of him was detached.

'Babies are surprisingly resilient,' she reassured the woman. 'And we're going to check him very carefully.'

Daniel conducted a thorough examination and Stella knew that he'd shut the conversation out of his mind with ruthless efficiency. He was looking for clinical signs that might suggest a problem. He wasn't thinking about babies or emotion.

He was palpating Fiona's abdomen when she gave a little gasp of fright and shifted on the trolley.

'Oh!' Her eyes widened with panic. 'I think I'm bleeding. Oh, God, am I losing it? Please don't say I'm losing the baby.'

More comfortable with a medical emergency than an emotional one, Daniel was cool and calm as he examined her. 'Stella—give my brother a call, will you? Tell him I need him down here.'

Meeting his gaze briefly, Stella moved to the phone and spoke to Switchboard.

Fiona put her hand over her eyes and started to cry. 'I can't believe I'm bleeding. I wish I'd never left the house. We were going Christmas shopping. I know there's another three weeks to go but I wanted to get it out of the way in case something happens. And now I've made it happen.' Great tearing sobs shook her body and Stella slipped her arm around the woman's shoulders, trying to imagine how she'd feel in the same position.

'You haven't made anything happen,' she soothed. 'You must try and calm down, for the baby's sake.'

'If I lose this baby—'

'Fiona.' Daniel reached for an IV tray, nothing in his voice betraying the fact that he was concerned. 'I want you to relax and trust me. My brother is one of the best obstetricians in the country and he will take a look at you.'

'*One* of the best?' Patrick strode into the room, a mocking gleam in his eyes as he looked at Daniel. 'I'm not one of the best. I'm *the* best.'

Fiona blinked in shock and Stella sighed.

'Yes, they're twins. Don't worry, you're not seeing double. Both of them as arrogant as the other.'

Fiona gave a feeble smile. 'Are they as good as they seem to think they are?'

'Fortunately, yes.' Stella adjusted one of the probes. 'Or maybe I should say *un*fortunately. I don't know. It makes them unbearable to be with, but I suppose it's good for the patients. Patrick? Do you want to take a look at this CTG trace?'

'I'm looking.' Patrick stood next to her, studying the trace in silence. 'All right—so there are a few dips there.'

Stella looked up and found Daniel glancing between her and Patrick. Then he focused on his brother's profile, so like his own. His jaw tightened, his blue eyes glittered dangerously and Stella felt a rush of trepidation. He'd obviously registered the fact that Patrick hadn't been surprised to see her.

Patrick looked up and met his brother's accusing gaze.

They were like a couple of stallions, Stella thought with exasperation, locked in a battle over territory. The interaction lasted less than a few seconds, but the impact was sufficiently powerful to leave her nervous of what was to come.

Why couldn't she have fallen in love with someone mild and gentle?

Pivoting back to the patient, Daniel fastened a tourniquet around Fiona's arm. 'I'm just going to put a cannula in your vein, in case we need to give you some fluid. Can you straighten your arm for me?'

'Stella—can I have a pen?' While Daniel set up an IV, Patrick was examining the woman's abdomen. 'I want to mark the height of her uterus.'

Stella swiftly provided him with a pen, wishing she'd never accepted Patrick's offer of accommodation. It was going to cause problems, just as she'd feared. She should have stayed somewhere else.

Then she frowned, cross with herself. The stable was lovely. And she could live anywhere she chose to live. It was none of Daniel's business.

And if it was difficult for him—well, tough. *He didn't care, did he?*

'Why are you drawing on me?' Fiona looked at Patrick anxiously and he slipped the pen into his pocket.

'You've had some blood loss. It's possible for some of the blood loss to be concealed, trapped behind the uterus. I want to make sure your uterus isn't bigger than it should be. Dan, is there anything else I should know about? Any neck injury? Spine?'

'No.'

'Then I want her nursed in the left lateral position.'

'Fine. I'm nearly done here.' Daniel filled the necessary bottles and dropped them on the tray.

Stella stepped forward and helped him connect the IV, the casual brush of his arm against hers sending a shower of sparks over her.

And he noticed her reaction.

His eyes shifted to her face. As a doctor, he was trained to detect changes in the human body and he was a man who knew women. A man who knew *her.*

'Everything all right?'

'Everything is fine,' she said sweetly, wishing he wasn't quite so astute. Nothing passed him by. Nothing. And as much as she'd hoped that working together would be smooth and easy, it was turning out to be anything but.

Focusing on the pain that went alongside loving Daniel Buchannan, Stella murmured words of comfort to Fiona and helped her turn on her side.

'Why do I have to lie like this?'

'Because lying flat on your back puts pressure on one of your major blood vessels and that's not good for the baby.' Patrick checked the baby's heart rate. 'That's better. Thanks, Stella. That's great.'

Daniel shot him a look. 'It's good to have Stella back, isn't it?' There was an edge to his tone that wasn't lost on his brother.

'Definitely.' Playing with fire, Patrick smiled. 'I was so pleased when she called me to talk through her plans.'

Stella threw him an incredulous glance. What was he doing? He appeared to be asking for a black eye for Christmas.

'You didn't mention it.' Daniel adjusted the IV. 'It must have slipped your mind.'

'Nothing slips my mind. I just didn't think you'd be interested.' Calmly, Patrick checked the monitor. 'What bloods have you taken?'

'U&Es, FBC, cross-match, BMG, coagulation screen, rhesus and antibody status and Kleihauer—why? Did I miss something?'

'No.' Ignoring the snap in his brother's tone, Patrick winked at the patient. 'Now he'll be unbearable.'

Fiona shifted the oxygen mask slightly. 'Twins, both of you doctors.' She sounded amazed. 'One

of you is an emergency specialist and one of you
is an obstetrician?'

'That's right. My brother is the emergency specialist.' Patrick looked at Daniel. 'The work suits
his personality. Quick and dirty. All superficial,
no depth or emotion.'

Daniel's firm mouth flickered into a smile.
'That's how I prefer it.'

While they bantered, the two brothers
worked together seamlessly, exchanging information, conducting tests. Then Patrick moved
to the side of the trolley and put his hand on
Fiona's shoulder.

'Fiona, I think there could be some concealed
bleeding behind your uterus.' He spoke gently,
knowing that the news he was giving wasn't
going to be well received. 'At the moment everything is fine and I'm not going to interfere, but I
want to transfer you to the labour ward, just to
be safe. We can monitor you there and if we
need to intervene, we can.'

Fiona shifted on the trolley. 'What's causing
the bleeding?'

'It's possible that a small part of the placenta
has come away from the uterus—we call it an

abruption. I want to keep you in hospital for now, see how things develop.'

Fiona swallowed. 'And if it gets worse?'

'Then I will deliver your baby.'

'But the baby isn't due until January.' Panic drove her voice up a pitch. 'I have another six weeks to go.'

'All the indications are that the baby is fine,' Patrick said calmly. 'And thirty-four weeks is early, that's true, but not so early that I'd be worried. We have an excellent special care baby unit here—we call it the SCBU—but at thirty-four weeks your baby might not need any extra help. Let's see how you go. My plan is to keep him inside you as long as possible.'

Fiona's face crumpled and she started to cry again. 'But this wasn't *my* plan. I've been reading all the books—I've gone to all the classes—I know exactly how I want my labour to be.'

Stella picked up a box of tissues, about to intervene, but Patrick took Fiona's hand in his. 'It's hard when things don't go according to plan,' he said gruffly. 'I really understand that. It happened with Posy, my youngest, and it shook me up. Nightmare. Nature has a way of keeping us all on our toes, but all that really matters is that the baby is safe, Fiona. Remember that.'

'Babies can die if they're premature.'

'There is no evidence that your baby is in trouble. And from now on I'm going to be watching you.' Patrick pulled a couple of tissues from the box Stella was holding and handed them to Fiona. 'Once you have kids, life rarely goes according to plan. Chaos is part of the fun. Or that's what I tell myself when I'm tripping over children, kittens and unwrapped Christmas presents.'

Stella felt a lump in her throat. Tripping over children, kittens and unwrapped Christmas presents sounded like paradise to her. 'Is there anyone else I can call for you, Fiona?' Stella yanked her mind back from its fruitless journey towards a dead end. 'Your husband is just having a few stitches in his head and then I'll bring him to wherever you are.'

'I keep thinking that this is all my fault. Perhaps I shouldn't have worn the seat belt—'

'Wearing a seat belt is the right thing to do,' Daniel said firmly. 'Contrary to popular opinion, wearing a seat belt does lower the risk of serious injury. Fiona, just relax and trust us. Patrick will make whatever decision needs to be made and it will be the right one, believe me.'

Patrick lifted his eyebrow. 'You're saying I'm always right?'

Despite her tears, Fiona gave a choked laugh. 'Are they always like this?'

'No, sometimes they're really bad,' Stella said cheerfully, squeezing Fiona's hand. 'I'll come with you up to the ward. Then I'll go and check on your husband. He must be worried sick.'

'He feels horribly guilty, but it wasn't his fault. The roads are lethal.'

'I'll go and see him as soon as we've settled you upstairs,' Stella assured her. 'Is there anyone else I can call?'

Fiona closed her eyes. 'My mum? No, not my mum. You'll just worry her. No one for the time being. But thanks. You've all been really kind.'

'Let's get you upstairs.' Patrick moved the trolley towards the door and Daniel's gaze settled on his face.

'I want to talk to you.'

Patrick smiled. 'I bet you do. But I'm busy, so it's going to have to wait.'

* * *

Daniel strode down the corridor, his tension levels in the danger zone after six hours of working shoulder to shoulder with Stella. Six hours of torture. At one point she'd leaned forward to pass him an instrument and he'd detected the faint smell of roses. Knowing that it was the shampoo she always used had set up a chain reaction in his brain. Thinking about the shampoo had made him think about her hair, long and loose. And thinking about her hair long and loose had made him think about her in his bed. And thinking about her in his bed had—

Daniel ruthlessly deleted that thought from his mind, but it immediately popped back again, taunting and teasing his senses until he gave a low growl of frustration, oblivious to the pretty nurse who gazed at him as she hurried past.

Without slackening his stride, he took the six flights of stairs up to the obstetric unit, too impatient to wait for the lift.

Nodding briefly to a consultant he knew, he made straight for his brother's office and pushed open the door.

'You knew Stella was coming back and you didn't tell me?'

Patrick leaned back in his chair and lifted an eyebrow. 'Next time, knock. I could have had a naked woman in here.'

Daniel planted his hands on the edge of his brother's desk, struggling with his temper. 'Damn it, Patrick—just how long have you been communicating with my ex-girlfriend?'

Patrick closed the file he'd been reading. 'Your ex-*fiancée*,' he said with gentle emphasis, 'and I've been "communicating" with her since you unceremoniously dumped her. On Christmas Eve. Not exactly the present she'd been hoping for, I'm sure.'

Daniel felt a sudden rush of cold. 'Why are you bringing that up now? That's history.'

'If it's history, why are you standing in my office threatening me?'

Daniel dragged his hand through his hair. 'I didn't dump her. She dumped me.'

Patrick stood up abruptly, impatience making his eye flash a deep blue. '*After* you told her you wouldn't marry her.'

'Not wouldn't—*couldn't*. It isn't that I don't

want to get married,' Daniel said hoarsely, 'I do. But I *can't*. I just can't do it. I would make a lousy husband and a terrible father and I won't do that to a child.' Sweat tingled on his brow as he thought of how close he'd come to breaking his promise to himself. Only Stella could have driven him to that. 'I can't be what she wants me to be. I did it for her.'

'Funny. She didn't appear that grateful last time I looked.'

'She should be grateful. Better to let her down now than in five years' time.' Or at least, that's what he'd told himself when he'd driven the scalpel through her heart.

Trying to dispel that image, Daniel pressed his fingers into the bridge of his nose and Patrick sighed.

'Why would you have let her down?'

'Being a mother is really important to Stella. Sometimes I think it's the only thing that matters to her.' Trying to get a grip on his emotions, Daniel clamped his hands over the edge of Patrick's desk. 'And I knew I couldn't be what she wanted me to be. She has this picture in her head—the perfect family. Mum,

Dad, lots of kids—probably a dog or two.' He gritted his teeth. 'And I'm not the guy in that picture. Fatherhood is the one job I'm not going to try. You mess that up, you take people with you.'

'I happen to think you wouldn't mess it up,' Patrick replied calmly, 'but I know you believe it. Which is why I didn't knock your head off two years ago.'

Daniel straightened. 'So you agree I did the right thing.'

'No. But I know you think you did. And I didn't want to watch you self-destruct and take Stella with you. She is a rare, special person. The sort of woman who would be by your side no matter what life throws at you. She wants marriage and a family—and she'll make someone a fantastic wife and mother.'

'And is that "someone" going to be you?' Anger roared through him like fire through a parched forest and Daniel strode around the desk and grabbed his brother by the shoulders. 'You're in need of a wife and a mother for your children—is Stella going to fill that slot? Is that why she's back?'

Patrick didn't flinch. 'You've just said you're not interested. Why would you care?'

'I never said I didn't care.' Daniel let his hands drop, stunned by his own reaction. *Since when had he picked fights with his twin?* 'I just don't think you're the right man for Stella.'

'I don't think you're qualified to judge. Relationships aren't your speciality, are they?'

Daniel stared at his brother for a long moment and then breathed out slowly. 'You're not having a relationship, are you? You're just winding me up.'

'Why would that wind you up? You decided you're not good for Stella. Right or wrong, that means she's free to be with another man. And with her long legs and her sweet nature, they're going to be beating her door down. You'd better get used to it.'

Sweat pricking his forehead, Daniel tried to imagine getting used seeing Stella with another man. 'That's fine. No problem. I just don't want her mixed up with someone unsuitable. She's pretty innocent.'

'She went out with you for two years,' Patrick reminded him dryly, 'so she can't be that innocent.'

Thinking about the steam and sizzle that had

characterised their relationship, Daniel suddenly felt a rush of dangerous heat. The thought of Stella with another man made his stomach churn. 'I just don't want some man messing her around.'

'Like you did? Don't worry—if she survived you, she'll survive anyone.' Patrick strolled back to his desk and sat down. He took a set of notes from a pile and reached for a pencil. 'I need to do some work.'

'Why is she back?'

'Obviously she's got over you and felt able to come home. She has friends here.' Patrick scanned some results, scribbled something onto the notes and dropped them in a tray ready to be collected. 'A life.'

A life that didn't include him. 'And you're one of those friends?'

'Of course. I've known her as long as you have. She was my friend, as well as yours. She made Christmas for us that year you and Carly had your own mini-meltdowns.' He looked at Daniel, a warning in his gaze. 'I'll never forget how she picked herself up and got on with things. Her heart was breaking but she still managed to dance around the house wearing antlers to make my son laugh.'

'She was always good with children. That was our problem. All Stella ever wanted was children.' *And children were the last thing he wanted.* Daniel stared at the row of photographs of his niece and nephew that Patrick had hung on the wall. Alfie and Posy giggling on a sledge. The two of them covered in ice cream at the beach. Posy in a backpack, grabbing Patrick's hair. 'Those two human beings are totally reliant on you. If you screw up, they suffer.'

'Thanks for that vote of confidence.'

'Doesn't it terrify you?'

'No. I love them. And I don't intend to screw up.' Patrick toyed with the pencil. 'It doesn't have to be the way it was for us, Dan.'

It was something they rarely mentioned and Daniel felt the filthy sludge of the past slide into his brain. 'Christmas was the worst time, do you remember?'

The pencil in Patrick's lean fingers snapped in two. 'Yes.'

'I counted the days until it was over.'

'I counted them with you.' His brother's casual tone didn't fool him and suddenly Daniel wanted to know.

'So how have you managed to put it behind you? With that grim example of parenting shining in your head, how do you do it?'

'I love my children.' A faint smile touched his brother's mouth. 'And I suppose I treat our childhood as an education in how not to parent. As long as I'm doing everything opposite, then I'm pretty confident that it will turn out all right.'

'You're divorced.'

'Precisely. If Mum and Dad had divorced, they might have been happy.' Patrick threw the broken bits of pencil into the bin. 'I don't subscribe to the school of thought that says a miserably unhappy couple have to stay together for the sake of the children. Why are we talking about this? What does this have to do with Stella?'

'I'm reminding you why I don't want marriage.'

'I don't need reminding.'

'I did her a favour.'

'You truly believe that, don't you?' Patrick gave a humourless laugh. 'Dan, you proposed to her and then broke her heart. What I don't understand is why you asked her to marry you in the first place, given your serious allergy to that condition.'

Daniel ran his hand over the back of his neck,

remembering that night. 'It was Christmas. I was crazy about her. It was what she wanted.'

'But not what *you* wanted.'

'For a brief moment I thought I did,' Daniel confessed in a raw tone. 'I thought maybe, just maybe, I could do it, but when your Carly—' Breaking off, Daniel threw his brother a glance of apology but Patrick shrugged.

'Don't mince your words. When Carly walked out on me, it reminded you that relationships are difficult, fragile things.'

'And Alfie cried himself to sleep at night for months!' Daniel's eyes slid to the photographs on the wall. 'I never want to do that to a child.'

Patrick eyed the stack of work on his desk. 'Could we talk about this in my kitchen over a beer later? Or was there something else you wanted to say?'

Daniel tried to clear his head. 'You should have told me that she was coming back.'

'I didn't think you'd be interested. You're dating that sleek, sexy solicitor, remember? You've moved on.' Patrick closed the file he'd been reading and placed it in a tray at the front of his desk ready to be collected.

Glaring at his brother, Daniel wondered how it was possible to love a person and hate them at the same time. 'Well, how long is she back for? Where is she living?'

'As far as I know, she's back for good.' Patrick leaned back in his chair and looked his brother in the eye. 'And she's living with me.'

CHAPTER TWO

STELLA walked into the treatment room and stopped the moment she saw Daniel. Her stomach flipped and her heart did a crazy dance. 'Sorry, I just needed to pick up a dressing pack.' Depressed by the effect he had on her, she backed towards the door and then noticed that he was putting an ice pack on his knuckles. 'Have you hurt yourself? What happened?'

'I hit my hand on something.'

Forgetting her own feelings for a moment, Stella stared at his profile, sensing his boiling anger. She knew him so well. Understood his moods, his volatility and his restless, brilliant mind. She remembered Patrick once telling her that if Daniel hadn't suddenly decided to be a doctor, he probably would have ended up in gaol. 'You hit your hand? Oh, God.' Her stomach lurched as the truth hit her. 'You've seen Patrick, haven't you? Please tell me you didn't—'

'No.' He growled the word angrily as he flexed his fingers. 'I didn't. Believe it or not, I have no intention of adding grievous bodily harm to my list of sins. I punched the wall.'

'Oh.' Relief poured over her. 'What had the wall done wrong?' But even while she was making a joke of it, her thoughts were spinning all over the place. This was because of her, she had no doubt about that. And part of her felt light-headed that her arrival had destabilised him because it meant that he still *cared*. And another part was angry with herself because that reaction was so infuriatingly illogical. She didn't want him to care for her and she didn't want to care for him.

She'd been there. Done that. Tested their relationship to the limits.

Watched it snap.

The glance he threw in her direction was dark and threatening. 'This isn't funny.'

'I agree.' *If they couldn't put the past behind them it certainly wasn't going to be funny.* Crisp and professional, Stella walked over to him and took his hand in hers, examining the bruising.

But she found herself thinking about the strength in those fingers—the skill she knew he possessed. Skill in the resuscitation room. *Skill in the bedroom.* 'That's a nasty bruise.' Taking the ice pack from him, she repositioned it so that it rested on the worst of the bruising. 'I suppose I should be relieved that you've learned to hit the wall and not your brother, otherwise I would have had both of you in here and that would take some explaining. Are you going to have this X-rayed?'

'What for? Nothing's broken.' There was a rough note to his voice that told her he was as aware of her as she was of him. 'Who's the doctor here?'

'You are.' She was tempted to slide the ice pack down the front of her scrub suit to cool her over-heated body. 'But you don't appear to be thinking clearly.' And she wasn't thinking clearly, either, with him so close to her. Suddenly holding his hand didn't seem like such a clever idea. The sight of those dark hairs shading his strong forearms was enough to make her think things she shouldn't be thinking and the sudden flare of sexual awareness was like a punch to her senses. Stella let go of his hand. 'I'll get you a bandage.'

'I don't need a bandage.'

'Then maybe you need an MRI to look at brain function,' she said tartly, her tone reflecting her frustration with herself. 'Going around hitting walls isn't exactly the behaviour of a consultant.'

'I wasn't a consultant when I punched the wall. I was a man. Dammit, Stella.' He caught her chin in his undamaged hand, turning her face to his, his movements strong and confident, his tone raw and demanding. 'Why didn't you tell me you were coming back?'

The way he touched her rattled her self-control. 'I didn't think you needed to know.'

'But you told my brother.'

'Yes.'

'You're living with him.'

Stella moved her head but he had her trapped. 'Not *with* him. In the stable. Is that why you tried to knock a hole in the wall?' Watching his reaction, she shook her head in disbelief. 'For goodness' sake, Daniel! What is the matter with you? I've seen you handle drunks and drug addicts with calm and patience. I've seen you ice cold, resuscitating a newborn baby when the other doctors in the room were all shaking hands and sweating brows. You have more control than any other man I know. And more intelligence.'

'He said you were living with him.'

'*In the stable!* Can't you tell when he's winding you up?'

Daniel gave a grunt and let his hand drop. 'My brother knows which buttons to push.'

'You two don't change.' But she knew how close they were and felt a flash of guilt for causing friction. 'There's nothing between Patrick and me.'

'It's two years since Carly walked out. He's ready for another relationship.' His tone was rough. 'If that's what the two of you want, I'm relaxed about it.'

Relaxed?

Stella decided not to remind him that his knuckles had required an ice pack. It was natural, she told herself, that he'd feel uncomfortable about her being with Patrick. It was just too close for comfort. He was probably worried that he'd be tripping over her every time he called in on his brother. 'Is that what you're buying him for Christmas? A relationship?'

Daniel flexed his fingers, testing the injury. 'I

think we both know relationships aren't my speciality. And you still haven't answered my question. Why are you back?'

'I'm back because this is where I want to live, Daniel! I love the Lake District—I love the hospital. My friends are here. The only reason I went away in the first place was because I just couldn't work alongside you after everything that happened. But I've moved on.' She hoped she sounded convincing. 'And so have you. If you're worried about awkward moments, then don't be. There won't be any.'

'Have you moved on?'

'Of course.' Stella thought of 'Caring of Cumbria'.

'That Christmas two years ago—'

'Let's not talk about it. There's no point.' Surprised and unsettled by his unexpected reference to their highly emotional break-up, Stella decided that the best thing was to show him everything was fine. 'I hear you're seeing someone. That's good. I'm pleased for you.'

Daniel discarded the ice pack. 'You are?'

'Of course. I only ever wanted you to be happy. I'm seeing someone, too.'

Daniel inhaled sharply and his eyes narrowed to two dangerous slits. 'Who?'

Stella suddenly realised that she didn't want to tell him she was using a dating agency. Why did that feel embarrassing? She didn't know, but it did. 'Just a guy.'

'So you don't know him very well.'

'That's why we're dating. To get to know each other.'

'How long have you known him?'

Stella was starting to wish she'd never begun the conversation. 'A couple of months.' Which was true, she reasoned. They'd been emailing each other since October.

'What does he do?'

'What does it matter?' She stared at him, exasperated and confused. 'Why do you care?'

'I'm just making conversation. Finding out what's been happening to you.' But the expression in his eyes said differently. 'Isn't that what friends do?'

'Yes, but we're not friends, Dan,' Stella said softly. 'We haven't been in touch for two years and I think we both know that was the right decision.' *Staying in touch would have been like squeezing lemon juice onto an open wound.*

'You don't seem to have any problems being friends with my brother.'

'Patrick and I have only ever been friends.'

'Whereas you and I were lovers.'

His husky, sexy voice sent a white hot arc of sexual heat shooting through her body and Stella felt everything inside her melt. 'It's in the past, Dan.' She stepped back, rejecting the fiery chemistry and her body's instinctive response. 'It's not going to give us a problem.' Picking up the equipment she'd come to fetch, she walked back towards the door. 'We're colleagues, that's all.'

'So you can work side by side with me and not feel anything.'

'That's right.' The lie came easily, but they were wasted words because both of them knew the truth. 'We want different things.' It seemed like a good idea to remind them both of that fact.

'Are you going to marry him?'

Stella opened the door. 'I don't know.' That was true, she reasoned. She didn't know. 'And I don't understand why you would even care.'

'Are you having sex with him?'

'For goodness' sake, Dan!' With a gasp, she

pushed the door closed again, hoping that none of her colleagues had been walking along the corridor at that point. 'What business is that of yours?' Her eyes clashed with the burning fire of his and, for a moment, he didn't reply.

Then he drew in an uneven breath. 'None,' he said hoarsely, running his undamaged hand through his hair like a man on the edge. 'None at all. And if you are—well, I'm fine with it. That's fine.'

Desperately unsettled, Stella held his gaze, not understanding what was going on in his head. They hadn't spoken to each other for two years. He was seeing someone else. There was no reason for him to react with anything other than indifference.

Except that their relationship had been so hot and intense that it had left scorch marks on both of them.

'I'm glad you're fine with it,' she said shakily, 'because who I date is none of your business. Just as who you date is none of mine.' Deciding that she'd never understand men, Stella left the room before she said something she knew she'd regret.

* * *

'So you've never met this person? How do you know he's nice?' Alfie was kneeling on a chair in the stable, watching Stella as she tapped away at the computer. One of the kittens was snuggled on his lap.

'We've been writing to each other.'

'By email?' Alfie looked knowledgeable. 'I have my own email address at school.'

'Really? That's impressive. I certainly didn't know how to email when I was ten years old.' Stella scrolled through her latest message, scanning the contents. 'He wants to meet me, Alfie. What do you think?'

'Let's ask Mary.' He lifted the tiny kitten. 'What do we think, Mary?'

'You called the kitten Mary?'

'It's Christmas. The two I'm keeping are Mary and Joseph. They're the marmalade ones.' He kissed the kitten on the head and rubbed his cheek over the animal's fur. 'It isn't safe to meet a stranger. My teacher says you should never give anyone your real name or address over the internet.'

'Your teacher is right. You shouldn't.' Stella typed her reply. 'And I haven't given any personal details apart from my name. He wants to meet me in a pub.'

Alfie stroked the kitten. 'What if you meet him and he's, like, *really* yucky?'

'Well.' Stella didn't reveal that she'd been wondering that exact thing herself. 'I hope he won't be. We've already talked about the things we like and don't like. So we have a feel for whether we're going to get on.'

'You mean you tell him you like computer games and he tells you he likes playing with Lego?'

'Something like that.'

'What if he's lying just so that you'll be friends with him?'

Stella lifted her hand and ruffled his hair. 'Smart, aren't you?'

'Not really. Harry Trent did that to me,' Alfie grumbled. 'He said he loved Lego, so I invited him to my house for a sleepover but when he got here he just wanted to nose around. And he kept asking questions about how much money Dad has. He wasn't interested in Lego.'

'I'm sorry to hear that,' Stella said softly. 'And if this guy is lying to me, I won't see him again.'

'Why can't you just meet someone normally?

It's going to be *really* weird going out with someone you've never met.'

'Sometimes it's hard meeting someone "normally".' Stella stroked the kitten gently. 'We lead busy lives and the chances of just bumping into someone you want to spend the rest of your life with are pretty remote.'

'Why can't you just be with Uncle Dan? You were going to marry him. Two Christmases ago you sat on my bed and read me that story and you showed me the ring Uncle Dan had given you.'

Remembering how quickly her best Christmas had turned into her worst Christmas, Stella bit her lip. 'We managed to have fun that Christmas despite everything, didn't we?'

'Oh, yeah.' Alfie shrugged, more adult than child. 'It was hard at first, when Mum left. Christmas was the final straw for her. She was screaming and yelling like she'd gone mad. At first I thought it was my fault for opening one of my presents early, but Dad told me it was his fault for going to deliver those triplets on Christmas Eve when Mum had dinner on the table.'

'I remember the triplets. Your dad saved their lives.'

'I know. He's cool. But Mum didn't think so. She hated his job. And she hated Christmas.' Alfie looked puzzled. 'I don't get that, do you? How can anyone hate Christmas? Dad says it stressed her out.'

Finding it hard to feel sympathy for a woman who could leave her children on Christmas Eve, Stella leaned forward and hugged him tightly. 'Alfie…' she discovered that she had a huge lump in her throat '…this Christmas is going to be the best ever. I promise. And no one is going to be stressed out.'

'If Dad has to cook a turkey, *he'll* be stressed out,' Alfie predicted, with insight beyond his years. 'And I'll probably be stressed out if I have to eat it. Dad is better at delivering triplets than cooking. He needs lessons. He's going to advertise for someone who wants a kitten. Do you think I could advertise for someone to come and cook Christmas lunch?'

'You don't need to advertise. I'll give him a lesson,' Stella promised, kissing him on the forehead and then pulling a face. 'Sorry—are you too old to be kissed?'

'I don't mind it,' Alfie said generously, 'as long as you don't do it in front of my friends.'

'I'll remember that.' Stella shut down her computer. 'Have you made your Christmas list?'

'Yes. And I've posted it up the chimney.'

Stella looked at him, unsure whether he still believed in Father Christmas. 'And did he pick it up?'

'It wasn't there when I looked so, yes, I guess so.' He picked up the tiny kitten and kissed it. 'I hope no one wants the kittens. Then we'll have to keep all of them.'

'It would be a lot of work for your dad.'

'I take care of them.' Alfie tucked the kitten back on his lap. 'I wish you'd married Uncle Dan.'

Stella thought, *Me, too,* but managed a smile. 'Your Uncle Dan isn't the marrying kind.'

'I know. He thinks marriage sucks.'

Stella blinked. 'Are you supposed to use that word?'

'Probably not, but I know you won't tell.' Alfred slid off the chair. 'If you don't want to marry Uncle Dan, you could always marry my dad. Then you could cook the turkey. And be my mum. That would be cool.'

'Being your mum would be cool,' Stella agreed, closing her laptop. 'But unfortunately your dad and I don't love each other. Not in that way. And people who get married should love each other.'

'You'd have to have sex, and I guess that would be gross.'

Stella gulped. 'Alfie!' she floundered, not sure how to respond, but Alfie had already moved on.

'What's his name? This guy you're meeting?'

'Edward.'

Alfie wrinkled his nose. 'I don't like that name.'

'It's just a name, Alfie.'

'Does he drive a cool sports car like Uncle Dan?'

'I have no idea.'

'Is he in the mountain rescue team like Dad and Uncle Dan?'

'I don't think so.'

'I'm going to be in the mountain rescue team when I'm old enough. I think it's *so* great, going out into the mountains to save people. You get to slide down ropes and sometimes go in a helicopter. I'm going to get muscles like Dad and Uncle Dan.'

Dismissing a disturbing mental image of Daniel's muscular physique, Stella gave a weak smile. 'I'm sure you will.'

'Last winter he went all the way to South

America and climbed a mountain no one else has ever climbed. How cool is that?'

'Pretty cool.'

'Does your guy climb?'

Stella took a deep breath. 'He isn't my guy and, no, he doesn't climb.'

'He sounds a *lot* different from Uncle Dan.'

'Yes,' Stella said breezily. 'He is.'

She was counting on it.

CHAPTER THREE

THE weather grew colder still and the emergency department was busier than ever.

Which was good, Stella reminded herself as she worked her third double shift with no break, *because work took her mind off Daniel.*

'I've never had a headache like it,' the woman moaned, holding her head as Stella checked her blood pressure. 'It feels as though someone is splitting my skull with an axe. We saw the GP yesterday and he said that we've all picked up this virus that's going around, but today when I woke up I felt so bad I was scared I was having a stroke or something.'

'The whole family has had the same bug?'

'My husband John has been really sick, but he had the headache, too. And the kids feel rough. They're supposed to be doing nativity plays and Christmas parties but they're too ill to be excited about anything. I left them sleeping this morning. Billy wouldn't even wake up when I went to tell him I was coming here and he's usually the first one up in the morning.'

'He wouldn't wake up?' Stella recorded the woman's blood pressure, but something in the patient's story made her uneasy. 'Are you sure? Did you try waking him?'

'Yes. This bug has totally wiped him out, poor thing.'

Stella looked at her for a moment, a suspicion forming in her mind. 'And your husband?'

'He was asleep, too. I wanted him to drive me here,' Diana muttered, 'but I couldn't even rouse him so I had to catch the bus. Still, I suppose he needed the rest after being sick yesterday.'

'Perhaps.' Stella glanced at the clock. 'What time did you leave the house?'

'An hour ago. Eight o'clock.'

'Right. Just wait there—I'm going to ask a doctor to take a look at you.' She hurried out of the cubicle and bumped straight into Daniel.

His fingers closed over her arms, steadying her. 'What's the rush? Or have you suddenly realised that there's only another twelve shopping days until Christmas?'

Stella didn't laugh, partly because she was too conscious of his hands on her body and partly because she was still distracted by her patient. 'I have a woman in cubicle 2 complaining of a severe headache.' She pulled away from him, alarmed that even when she was talking to him as a doctor, she was still aware of him as a man. 'The whole family is down with a virus.'

'And?' His gaze lingered on her face, dropped to her mouth. 'What are you thinking?'

That she must have been crazy to think she would ever get over Daniel. 'I'm thinking that it might not be a virus.' Yanking her mind back to her work, Stella gave an embarrassed laugh. 'I'm probably overreacting.'

'I've never known you overreact.' His voice was soft. 'I *have* known you see things other people miss.'

Stella was silenced by the praise. Thrown, it took her a moment to focus. 'She's had this headache for a while,' she croaked, looking past him down the corridor rather than at his face. 'Yesterday her husband and the kids were sick—'

'They saw their GP?'

'Yes, and he said virus. Gastroenteritis.'

'Sounds reasonable. There's plenty of it going around.'

'Yes.' Stella rubbed her fingers over her forehead and sighed. 'I'm definitely overreacting. If one member of the family has it then it's perfectly reasonable for the whole family to go down.'

Daniel's gaze was fixed on her face. 'Why are you worried?'

'Because when she left the house this morning she couldn't wake her kids or her husband. She thought they were just tired, but—'

'Are you telling me you think it might be carbon monoxide poisoning?'

'I hope not. I—I'm sure it isn't,' Stella stammered, suddenly feeling foolish. 'If it was just her husband who was tired, I wouldn't have been worried, but it's a bit odd not being able to wake a child who is normally bouncing around thinking of Christmas, don't you think?'

'How hard did she try?'

'I don't know.' Stella waved her hand. 'Will you take a look at her? See what you think? If there's a chance I might be right, we should call the police and the paramedics.' It occurred to her that she trusted his judgement implicitly. Whatever their differences, she'd never doubted his abilities as a doctor.

Daniel stared at her for a moment, his expression inscrutable. Then he turned and strode into the cubicle. 'Diane? I'm Daniel Buchannan, one of the consultants here. Tell me about your headache.' He questioned the woman as he examined her, his eyes sharp and attentive as he listened to the history and took some blood samples. 'And the other members of you family had nausea, vomiting and headache?'

'Yes,' she groaned, closing her eyes. 'I did wonder if it was something we'd eaten, but the GP said there is a gastric bug going around.'

'Her sats are fine,' Stella murmured, looking at the monitor.

'The saturation level equals the sum of oxyhaemaglobin and carboxyhaemoglobin, so it's unreliable. It isn't going to tell us what we want to know,' Daniel murmured. 'I want to give her the highest concentration of oxygen possible—use a rebreathing mask. I want to check her COHb levels. And let's do an ECG. Diane...' Daniel turned back to the patient '…I don't think this is a virus. I agree with Stella—I think you might have carbon monoxide poisoning.'

The woman looked at him blankly. 'What?'

'There's been quite a lot about it in the papers. It's a tasteless, odourless gas—it basically lowers the oxygen-carrying capacity of your blood. What sort of heating do you have at home?'

'We're in a rented flat,' Diane gasped. 'We have a gas fire in the living room. We tend to congregate there to save on heating bills. Do you think—?'

'I suspect that the fire might be a problem.'

'Oh, my God—the kids are in the house.' Panic flaring in her eyes, Diane struggled to sit up. 'My husband—'

'We're going to deal with it, Diane. Right now. Lie down and think about yourself for a moment.' Her tone soothing, Stella put the oxygen mask on the anxious woman, adjusted the flow to maximum and then looked at Daniel. 'Do you want me to call the house?'

'I'll do it. You do that ECG.'

Stella attached the leads to Diane's chest and had just switched the machine on when Daniel strode back into the room.

'Diane, there was no reply from your house,' he said gently, 'so I've called the fire brigade and the paramedics. It's just a precaution, but if we're right, we need to get the rest of your family in here as soon as possible.'

Diane's eyes were bright with tears. 'I had no idea! I just left them. I thought they were asleep!'

'We're getting someone round there now, Diane,' Stella said soothingly, but Diane just shook her head.

'What if it's too late?'

Daniel's mobile rang and he answered it swiftly, giving instructions to the paramedics.

'They're at the door now and there's no answer—is there a key anywhere?'

'Flower pot,' Diane murmured weakly, and Daniel relayed that message to the emergency services on the scene. Moments later he was nodding and smiling.

'You're sure? OK. Yes, I'll tell her that.' He dropped the phone into his pocket and smiled at Diane. 'Your husband is awake, Diane. They're getting the children out of the house now and they'll assess them in the ambulance.'

Diane closed her eyes briefly. 'Are they OK? Please tell me they're OK.'

'They're going to give them oxygen and transfer them straight to us.'

'Dan? Do you want to look at this ECG?' Stella stood to one side and Daniel scanned the strip of paper.

'That looks all right. Nothing there that worries me.'

'Why did that GP tell me it was a virus?' Diane fretted, and Daniel slipped the ECG reading into the notes.

'Unfortunately, it's all too easy to miss.'

'*You* didn't miss it.'

'We're a busy emergency department—we're more alert to the possibility of carbon monoxide poisoning than the average family doctor.'

'But if you hadn't thought of it—'

'You can thank this nurse.' Daniel's gaze slid to Stella. 'She was the one who was suspicious. And rightly so.' His eyes rested on her face for a moment and she smiled and then turned away, part of her wishing that they didn't work together so well. Maybe if she didn't admire him as much as a doctor…

A siren sounded outside the department and Daniel moved towards the door. 'That will be the rest of your family. I'll go and see to them and then I'll come back. Stella, if you need me, shout.' He strode out of the room, leaving Stella with a very worried Diane.

'Can I go and see them?'

'You're not well enough.' Stella encouraged her to stay on the trolley. 'Give Daniel time to assess them, and then I'll go and find out what is going on.'

But she didn't need to because Daniel walked into the room less than ten minutes later. 'I've done a preliminary examination and it does seem to be carbon monoxide poisoning, but they're going to be fine,' he assured Diane. 'Your husband is conscious and talking and the boys woke up once they were removed from the house. Your husband has contacted your landlord and the fire department will be dealing with him.' He checked the blood results. 'Her COHb levels are high,' he murmured to Stella. 'I'm going to talk to the infirmary—I'm wondering whether she would benefit from hyperbaric oxygen therapy.'

'I thought that was controversial?'

'I think it might be appropriate in Diane's case. I'll call them.' He strode out of the room again just as Ellie walked in.

'Diane? I've been looking after your lovely boys,' she said, 'and I wanted to let you know that they're doing fine. We've given them oxygen and they're sitting up and chatting. They've told me everything that's on their Christmas lists and all I can say is I hope you won the lottery recently.'

'They're all right?' Diane clutched Stella's hand. 'It's because of you,' she said hoarsely. 'It's because of you they're alive. I can't believe I just thought they were tired. You saved our lives.'

'She's a miracle,' Ellie agreed, winking at Stella, 'but don't tell her too often or she'll expect a pay rise and we don't do things like that around here.'

Stella smiled at her friend and squeezed Diane's hand. 'I'm just relieved that your family is all right.'

'If you hadn't thought of it—or if that doctor hadn't taken you seriously—'

'I always take her seriously,' Daniel drawled from the doorway, a gleam in his eyes as he glanced briefly at Stella. 'Diane, I've spoken to my colleagues and I'm transferring you for some special treatment, and the others, too.'

Stella helped with the arrangements and once Diane had been transferred, she went back to the room to clear up.

'Well done. You just made someone's Christmas.' Daniel stood in the doorway and her heart danced an uneven rhythm because the way he was looking at her was achingly familiar.

'I'm just glad it turned out all right.' She pushed the ECG machine to the end of the cubicle, reminding herself to keep it professional. If they just talked about work, it would be fine. 'How are the children? Ellie said they should be fine.'

'Their COHb levels were quite high, but hopefully they won't suffer any long-term problems. The fire brigade wore breathing apparatus when they went in. Apparently the gas fire was lethal. Blocked flue or something.' He strolled into the room, his eyes on hers. 'Good job, Stella. I've missed working with you.' His gruff male tones melted her bones to liquid.

'I've missed working with you, too,' she

breathed, her hands tightening around the side of the trolley. 'You're a good doctor.'

There was a painful silence and Stella stood there, so aware of him that he may as well have been touching her.

'Look at me, Stella.' His soft command made her heart skip and she lifted her head and looked at him. And instantly regretted it. With a murmur of confusion, she gave a little shake of her head and his eyes darkened.

'Stella, I—'

'Daniel?' A crisp, female voice came from behind him and they both glanced guiltily towards the door.

A woman stood there. She was slim and businesslike, dressed smartly in a navy suit and a white shirt, and in her right hand she held a briefcase. Her glossy red hair was neatly contained in a professional-looking French plait and her make-up was immaculate.

'Andrea.' Daniel hesitated and then cast a wary glance towards Stella.

And she understood instantly who the woman was.

His lawyer.

'I'll just go and check the waiting room.' Stella intended to slide out of the room, but the woman stopped her.

'Don't run away on my account. I'm due in court in ten minutes so I don't have long. Dan— about tonight. Don't pick me up. I'll meet you there. I'd rather drive myself.' She was all crisp efficiency. 'And I have a breakfast meeting tomorrow, so I won't be staying overnight.'

Stella dug her nails into her palms, horrified by the agonising pain she felt. She was supposed to be over him, wasn't she? *She wasn't supposed to care any more.* So why did it hurt to meet his latest girlfriend? And to hear her talking about 'staying over', as if it was a regular occurrence.

Well, of course it was. What had she expected? Daniel was a red-blooded male. Just because he had no interest in marriage and children, it didn't mean he had no interest in other things.

Shaken by the depth of the pain she felt, Stella mumbled an excuse and slid past the two of them, avoiding eye contact with Daniel.

He had his life and she had hers.

And that was the way she wanted it.

'Caring of Cumbria' was going to be her type,

she reminded herself. And he was going to stop her thinking about Daniel.

'What do you know about this guy she's seeing?' Daniel stood in his brother's kitchen, staring across the yard towards the converted stable. A light shone behind a curtain and he assumed that Stella was getting ready to go out for the evening. For some reason that he didn't understand, the thought set his teeth on edge.

'Nothing.' Patrick drained the pasta. 'Posy, sit at the table. Alfie, help your sister. God, I'm tired. I can't remember the last time I spent a whole night in my bed. The labour ward is crazy.'

'You're the boss. You're supposed to delegate.'

'I don't delegate life-and-death situations. Why are so many babies born near Christmas?'

'I don't know.' Daniel leaned forward and stole a piece of pasta. 'You're the obstetrician.'

'Can I have extra cheese on my pasta?' Alfie picked Posy up and sat her on her chair. Then he went to the fridge and pulled out a bottle of milk.

'Not milk,' Patrick said absently, cursing under his breath as the water scalded his fingers. 'Give her water. Otherwise she's too full to eat.'

Daniel felt something pressing on his ankle and looked down to see a kitten looking up at him hopefully. 'About this guy that Stella is seeing…'

'I don't know anything about the guy Stella is seeing.'

'I do.' Alfie replaced the milk and poured water into two cups. 'I know he's not in the mountain rescue team.' He put the cup in front of his sister. 'And I don't think he has muscles. But I know he wants to get married and have kids. That's why she's picked him. I just hope he doesn't turn out to be a real creep. She'll find out tonight. Ellie is going to phone her at nine and if he's really yucky then she's going to pretend there's a crisis at home. I guess that will work. She hasn't given him her address or anything.' He scooped up the kitten that was winding itself around Daniel's legs and sneaked it onto his lap under the table, casting a furtive glance at his father.

Stunned into silence by the volume of information that Alfie had delivered, Daniel gaped at his nephew and then turned to his brother. 'He's ten years old.'

'He inherited his intelligence from me.' Patrick

put a bowl of pasta in front of his golden-haired daughter. 'Alfie spends every available minute with Stella. He knows far more about her than I do.'

Daniel turned his attention back to his nephew. 'You've been spending time with her?'

'Why not? She's got this brilliant laptop. It's so cool. And she does this dating thing. You ought to do it, Dad.' Alfie squirted ketchup onto his plate. 'Stella had three hundred and fifty replies. If you had that many they could each come here and cook a meal and you wouldn't have to cook again for a whole year.'

'What's wrong with my cooking? And I know you've brought that kitten to the table again, Alfie. I'm not blind or stupid. Put her on the floor. And don't eat with your fingers, Posy.' Clearly distracted, Patrick put the fork into his daughter's hand. 'Alfie, eat, please. I've got to go back to the hospital in a minute.'

'Dating agency?' Feeling as though he was five steps behind everyone else, Daniel stared at his nephew. 'Stella is using a dating agency?'

'Yup.' Ignoring his father, Alfie kept the kitten on his lap. 'On the internet. It's the only way she's going to meet a decent man. She's been through three hundred and fifty people and she's chosen someone who isn't a bit like you.'

Patrick gave a choked laugh and Daniel glared at him and then pulled out a chair and sat down next to Alfie.

'So she's meeting a complete stranger?'

'Not really. She knows *loads* about him. I think he sounds really boring, but I'm not a girl.' Alfie stuffed a forkful of pasta into his mouth. 'She's really excited. Dad—how long does it take to make a baby?'

A baby?

Daniel had to physically stop himself from sprinting across the courtyard and bolting the stable door from the outside.

There was no way Stella would be intimate with a guy that quickly, he told himself. She wasn't that type of girl, was she? It had been ages before she'd eventually slept with him.

'Nine months,' Patrick said absently. 'Alfie, Mrs Thornton is going to sit with you tonight.'

Alfie groaned. '*Not* Mrs Thornton. She's so old.'

'She isn't old.'

'She smells funny and her mouth is really red. Can't I stay on my own?'

'You're too young. I won't be late.'

'You always say that, but babies are never predictable,' Alfie grumbled. 'They just don't do what you expect them to do. You'll be at the hospital all night, like you always are. If Mrs Thornton is here, can I watch that DVD? She's so short-sighted, she won't know.'

'Which DVD?' Only half listening, Patrick fished his mobile out of his pocket and scrolled through his messages.

'It's a twelve rating.'

'You're ten, so the answer is no.'

'My friends have all seen it.' Alfie wrinkled his nose. 'I don't think it's unsuitable.'

'So why is it a twelve rating?'

'Not sure. It will either be "scenes of a violent nature" or "moderate sex references".' Alfie spooned another pile of cheese over his pasta. 'It doesn't really matter. I fast forward those bits anyway. All that kissing is boring when you're ten.'

Patrick's phone rang and he answered it immediately. 'Buchannan. Yes. How many centimetres dilated is she?' Still listening, he tucked the phone between his cheek and his shoulder and wiped the tomato sauce from his daughter's face. 'No—no, not yet. All right.'

Alfie sighed. 'Wait for it. He's going to have to go to the hospital and sort it out.'

Daniel reached forward and stole a piece of pasta from Alfie's bowl. 'You know everything that's going on around here, don't you?'

'I have eyes and ears. Never underestimate a kid,' Alfie said solemnly, pulling his bowl out of Daniel's reach and wrapping an arm around it protectively. 'I have this whole house wired. I want to be a spy when I grow up. You could stay with me tonight, then Mrs Thornton wouldn't have to drag her creaking joints over here.'

'Creaking joints?' Daniel looked at his brother with disapproval, wondering who he was entrusting with his children. 'How old is this woman you're leaving him with?'

'At least forty-five,' Patrick drawled, sliding his phone into his pocket and removing the cheese from Posy's grasp. 'To Alfie, that's old.'

'She *is* old and she smells strong. And she's always asking about Daddy.'

'She covers herself in perfume before she comes round?' Daniel leaned back in his chair and grinned at his brother. 'Sounds as though she's interested in something other than the welfare of the children.'

'Unluckily for me.' Patrick scooped the kitten from Alfie's lap. 'Mary, go to the kitchen.'

'That's Joseph. I don't know how you can do your job if you can't tell the difference between a boy and a girl.' Alfie pushed his bowl away and looked at Daniel. 'Can't you stay with me tonight?'

'I have a hot date.' Glancing at his brother, who was still on the phone, Daniel leaned forward and lowered his voice. 'So, Agent Alfie, you wouldn't happen to know where Stella is meeting this mystery man of hers, would you?'

'Yes.' Alfie picked up his drink. 'I would.'

Daniel lifted an eyebrow. 'And are you going to tell me?'

'I might. But it's going to cost you.'

Daniel gave a disbelieving laugh. 'You think I'd pay you for information?'

'I suppose it depends how important it is to you.' Alfie slid off his chair and took his bowl to the kitchen.

Daniel followed. 'You're a tough negotiator.'

'You don't have to pay if you don't want to know.'

Out of his depth, Daniel took a deep breath and glanced through the door towards his brother, who was now on the phone again, talking to the hospital. 'How much is it going to cost me?'

Alfie set the dishwasher to rinse. 'Two pounds fifty.'

'That's daylight robbery.'

'Fine. Why do you want to know where she's going, anyway?' Alfie frowned. 'You two don't go out together any more. She thinks you're too macho and you're worried because she wants babies. I'm only ten but even I can see that that's going to be a terrible relationship. Kids are a lot of work. I know, because I am one.'

'She thinks I'm too macho?' Daniel ran his hand over the back of his neck, unable to believe that he was having this conversation with a ten-year-old. 'Where do you hear these things?'

'Stella talks to me. That's why I like her. She doesn't treat me like an idiot.'

'Alfie, you're no idiot.' Daniel dug his hand in his pocket and pulled out his wallet. 'Five pounds.'

Alfie's eyes widened. 'I don't have any change.'

'I want to know everything that Stella has told you about this guy.'

'All right.' Alfie folded the money carefully and tucked it in his pocket. 'They're meeting in the Drunken Fox at eight o'clock.'

'How are they going to recognise each other?'

'She's going to wear red.' Alfie pulled a face. 'I hope the guy likes red. She didn't know whether to wear the red one or the black one, but I said red because I thought she looked nicest in that one. Sort of like a girl from the movies.'

Daniel inhaled sharply. 'You should have gone with the black.'

'You don't want her to look nice?'

'Red is...' *The colour she'd always worn for him?* He'd loved her in red. For a moment his brain tortured him with a mini-clip of Stella in red. The soft red jumper she'd worn the first night he'd kissed her, the silky red dress she'd had on when he'd proposed. 'You should have told her to wear black.'

'Why? She looked better in the red.'

Precisely, Daniel thought viciously, searching

for an excuse to stride across to the stable, knock on the door and stop her going out.

'Why are you giving my son money?' Patrick ended the phone call and walked into the kitchen, Posy in his arms.

'I'm his uncle.' Daniel walked across and kissed Posy on the top of her head. 'I can give him money if I want to.'

Patrick's eyes narrowed suspiciously but at that moment the doorbell rang. 'That will be Mrs Thornton. Alfie, make sure you're in bed by eight-thirty. No messing around. And don't watch anything unsuitable.'

'Just go, Dad.' Alfie lowered the kitten gently to the floor and handed Posy her doll. 'We'll be fine. If Mrs Thornton dies of old age, I'll call you.'

'Don't be cheeky.'

Daniel walked towards the door. 'I'll catch you later.'

Patrick reached for his coat. 'Lucky you, having a night off. Are you seeing the lawyer?'

'Yes.' And Daniel strode out of the house before his brother could question him further.

For some reason he didn't want to examine

too closely, he wasn't prepared to tell Patrick how he planned to spend his evening.

Nodding to the woman on the doorstep, he made for his car.

CHAPTER FOUR

STELLA turned sideways and looked at herself in
the mirror. Was she overdressed? Perhaps she
should have just worn jeans. On the other hand,
if it went well they were going on to a restaurant
afterwards, so jeans might not be dressy enough.

She looked fine. It was just that the dress
reminded her of Daniel.

He'd always loved her in red and the last time
she'd worn this dress they'd—

Remembering what they'd done, Stella yanked
the dress over her head and threw it on the bed
with the other clothes she'd tried on. It was no
good. She couldn't wear it. It just felt wrong.
And the pile of clothes on the bed was growing.

Stella stared in the mirror, reminding herself that
this was a new relationship. A whole new chapter
of her life. And Daniel wasn't in her life any more.

And the fact that she couldn't stop thinking

about him made it even more important for her to go out with someone else.

Exasperated with herself, she grabbed the red dress again, relieved that no one was watching her. If anyone had seen how indecisive she was about a stupid dress, they'd fire her from her job.

She zipped it up a final time and then tried to do something with her hair, but there was so much static after all the clothes she'd pulled on and off over her head she just gave up in despair and left it loose.

Realising that she was going to be late if she didn't move fast, she eyed the clothes on the bed and decided she'd have to tidy them up later. Grabbing her favourite pair of black boots, she pulled them on and dragged her coat out of the wardrobe.

By her bed were various bags, filled with the beginnings of her Christmas shopping. Realising how much she still had left to do was enough to induce a panic attack, so she put the thought aside and reminded herself there was plenty of time until Christmas.

Fifteen minutes later she was in the car park of the pub, her heart thumping so hard she felt dizzy.

What if she knew someone in the pub?

She'd intentionally picked somewhere she didn't usually go, but this part of the Lake District was a relatively small community.

What if Alfie was right and Mr 'Caring of Cumbria' was a creep?

Feeling like turning round and driving straight home, it took all of her willpower to step out of the protective cocoon of her little car and walk across the icy car park to the small village pub.

What was the matter with her? It was just a drink, for goodness' sake. A drink and a meal. If it didn't work out, she wouldn't see him again.

As she pushed open the heavy door the warmth hit her and she felt daunted by the throng of people standing shoulder to shoulder at the crowded bar.

Deciding that she'd wait for it to calm down a bit before trying to buy herself a drink, Stella made her way to an empty table by the fire and slid discreetly onto the chair. Aware that everyone in the pub was staring at her, she wished she'd bought herself a drink. At least then she would have had something to do with her hands.

Feeling self-conscious, she removed her coat,

but left her scarf round her neck. Staring at the fire, she found herself thinking of Daniel. Then she realised that she didn't want to think about Daniel and gave herself a mental shake. She wasn't *allowed* to think about Daniel. The whole idea of this exercise was *not* to think about Daniel.

The door to the pub opened, letting in a rush of cold air and a flurry of snow. A short man in a pinstripe suit walked cautiously into the pub, snow clinging to his polished shoes. Hovering on the edges of a group of men dressed in thick cable knit jumpers and sturdy boots, he looked as out of place as a ballerina on Mount Everest.

Stella fought a sudden desire to whip off the red scarf she was wearing and slide under the table out of sight. She couldn't do that, could she? It would be rude. After agreeing to meet, the least she could do was have a drink with him.

But the thought of spending an evening with him made her feel so intensely gloomy that she contemplated texting Ellie and asking her to bring her emergency call forward by an hour.

Watching his tentative attempts to reach the bar, Stella couldn't help comparing him to Daniel.

Would this man be bold enough and strong enough to rescue a vulnerable child from a snowy ravine? Would he be cool and decisive enough to make life-and-death decisions, as Daniel did every day in the emergency department?

She turned her head away and stared at the fire, wondering why all the comparisons she was making were against Daniel's good points. Why couldn't she focus on his bad points? The man hovering nervously at the bar probably wouldn't propose to a woman one day and then change his mind a few hours later. The man at the bar was probably extremely patient with people less intelligent than him. He wanted children, and Daniel had made it clear that he had no intention of ever becoming a father. Those were the things she should be thinking about.

So why, knowing all that, was she still thinking of Daniel when she looked at the man at the bar?

The whole situation felt so hopeless that a lump formed in her throat. Getting over someone wasn't as easy as just finding someone else. It didn't work like that.

Stella slid her phone out of her pocket, intending to text Ellie and ask her to bring her call forward. But then a girl emerged from the crush at the bar and kissed the man on the cheek.

Feeling impossibly relieved, Stella put the phone back in her pocket.

All that worry and anxiety and it wasn't even him. But now she had a new worry.

What if he didn't turn up?

The door opened again and she glanced up expectantly.

Daniel stood in the doorway, flakes of snow clinging to his dark hair and broad shoulders, a dangerous look in his eyes.

'Dan.' The barman called out a greeting and Stella frowned slightly because she hadn't realised that he frequented this pub.

He said something that she didn't catch and glanced around the noisy pub.

Stella slid down in her seat and tried to be inconspicuous, but she knew it was hopeless. There was no way he could fail to spot her. He was going to want to know what she was doing here and she was going to have to confess that she was meeting a stranger. How sad was that? Not only had she had to resort to the internet to meet a man, but he hadn't turned up. Her confidence in herself suddenly evaporated.

She was unattractive and she was never going to meet anyone.

'Stella?'

Accepting the inevitable, she looked up at him.

Flakes of snow clung to his sleek dark hair and his jaw was dark with stubble. With the bulk of his shoulders and those long, strong legs, he looked strong, tough and imposing. A man who was afraid of nothing.

Nothing except commitment, Stella reminded herself wearily, producing what she hoped was a decent imitation of a smile. 'Hi, Daniel. This is a surprise. I thought you had a date with your lawyer at eight. You're going to be late. Will she sue you?'

He didn't laugh. In fact, he seemed a long way from laughing. 'What are you doing here on your own?' His ice-blue eyes glittered in the firelight and he pulled out a chair and sat down, nodding his thanks as the landlord discreetly placed a drink in front of him.

Stella fiddled with her scarf. 'They give you free drinks here?'

'His daughter fell in a climbing accident last summer. Nasty head injury. Tricky evacuation.'

'And you rescued her?'

'I was part of the team.'

Despite his concise, factual answer, Stella knew instinctively that he would have been the one to rescue the girl and manage the head injury.

'Have you had many callouts lately?'

'I don't want to talk about the mountain rescue team.' Daniel's eyes were fixed on her face. 'Tell me why you're here.'

That was the other thing about Daniel. He came straight to the point.

'I—I fancied a drink.'

'On your own?'

'No, not on my own. I was supposed to be meeting someone but he's been...' She licked her lips. 'He's been delayed.'

'Who are you supposed to be meeting? Your new boyfriend?'

Something in his tone made her look at him closely and she saw the tightness of his mouth and the deadly gleam of his eyes under the veil of thick, dark lashes. 'Why does it matter to you?'

'Because I don't think you should meet strange

men in pubs.' His tone abrupt and gritty, Daniel lifted his drink and Stella sensed that he knew.

He knew she was seeing someone she'd met on the internet.

Stella wondered why that felt so humiliating. 'Who told you?'

'That doesn't matter.' He put his drink down on the table with a thump. 'What matters is that you've arranged to meet a guy you don't know. Have you no sense of self-preservation?'

Startled by the anger in his voice, Stella looked at him. 'I'm in a crowded pub,' she said reasonably. 'What's going to happen?'

'He'll invite you back to his place and—' Daniel broke off, his eyes on her neckline.

'What?'

'You're wearing your red dress.'

'What's wrong with that?' Exasperated and self-conscious, Stella reached for her coat and pulled it on. 'I like this red dress. And I'm on a date. Go away and leave me alone, Daniel.' She'd hoped that the feelings she'd had for him had died, but she was fast discovering that life wasn't as simple as that.

'It isn't the right dress to wear with someone you've never met.'

'I wanted to look nice!'

'You're asking for trouble.'

'Well, it's hard to get into trouble with someone who hasn't even turned up.' Smarting with humiliation and anger, Stella picked up her bag and stood up. 'Thanks for the feedback, Dan.' Furiously angry with him, and with herself for caring what he thought, Stella walked quickly out of the pub.

The cold punched her in the face and she told herself that it was the weather that was making her eyes water as she picked her way across the icy car park towards her car. The temperature had dropped and a bitter wind breathed freezing air over her as she snuggled deeper inside her coat. Her windscreen was opaque with ice and she pulled a scraper out of her bag and attacked the ice, her fingers numb with cold as it showered over her hands. Scraping methodically, she wondered whether every Christmas was destined to be a romantic disaster for her.

Last Christmas she'd been working and the nearest she'd got to romance had been when a ninety-year-old patient had assured her that if he'd been six decades younger he would have married her. The Christmas before that—well, she wasn't even going to think about that one but this one didn't promise to be too much better.

The way the festive season was unfolding it looked as though she was going to need to stock up on comfort food.

As she pulled her car keys from her pocket and turned to unlock the car, her feet slid from under her and she would have fallen if strong hands hadn't caught her.

'Careful. It's icy.' Daniel's rough, masculine voice was next to her ear and she wrenched herself away from him.

'Let me go, Dan.' Terrified that she wasn't going to be able to hold it together, Stella shrugged him off with as much dignity as she could and opened her car door. 'I wish I could say it was nice bumping into you, but it wasn't.'

With a rough curse he turned her to face him, his hard, powerful body pressing her back against the cold metal of the car. 'Why are you meeting men on the internet?'

'Because I don't meet any decent ones in real life!' Her eyes clashed with his and then his hands slid into her hair and his mouth came down on hers.

It was so sudden and unexpected that she had no time to react.

The warmth of his mouth was such a contrast to the ice cold wind brushing her cheeks that she moaned in shock. And then she was responding to the seductive pressure of his kiss, her arms winding around his neck, her body trembling against his solid, masculine strength. His fingers tightened on her face, his kiss demanding and erotic as he created fire and flame with his mouth and tongue.

It was an explosion of pure sensuality, a heated, unfaltering, indulgent expression of passion that neither of them was able to halt.

And then the pub door opened behind them and the sound of laughter penetrated their sensual haze. Daniel tore his mouth from hers, swore fluently and stepped away from her. Raising his hands in a gesture of apology, he shook his head in disbelief, regret visible in his eyes. 'Stella, I didn't mean to—'

'Oh, get away from me, Dan,' she choked, sliding into the car and slamming the door, her body still reeling from that kiss. She didn't know which was worse—the fact that he'd kissed her or that fact that he hadn't meant to do it.

Damn, damn, damn. She should have pushed him away and showed him that she wasn't interested.

Why hadn't she done that?

Why hadn't she slapped his indecently handsome face?

Her hands shaking, she started the engine, crunched the gears, set the wipers going, skidded the car and then swung onto the road, desperate to get away from him.

Oh, God, she was going to have an accident if she carried on like this.

The knowledge that it would probably be Daniel who would patch her up if she was taken to the emergency department was enough of an incentive to make her slow her speed.

Fortunately the roads were deserted and she switched off the wipers that were moving snow across her windscreen and turned the heating as high as it would go.

What a total disaster.

The evening was supposed to have been the

first step in her Daniel Recovery Programme, instead of which she'd slipped right back into her old habits. It was like surviving an earthquake only to be trapped in a lethal aftershock.

It was *all* his fault. He was the one who had kissed her. Why couldn't he have just left her alone? Or why hadn't she slapped his face?

Furious with herself and even more furious with him, Stella crunched the gears again, tears blurring her vision as she drove down the narrow, empty roads that led to Patrick's barn.

It had been stupid to come back to the Lake District again. It was all very well having grand ideas about dating other men but the truth was she didn't *want* another man.

She wanted Daniel. She always had. And it didn't matter how unsuitable he was, she still wanted him. Patrick was right—love wasn't something you could switch on and off.

Her vision blurred and as she pulled into the courtyard of the barn, she almost crashed into the back of Patrick's car.

Slamming her brakes on just in time, the car slid to a halt a mere centimetre from his bumper and she switched off the engine and closed her eyes.

What next?

Her car door opened. 'Are you trying to kill yourself or me?' Patrick took one look at her frozen features and leaned across and undid her seat belt. 'Come on. You look as though you need a drink.'

'Actually, I don't need a drink.' Her teeth were chattering. 'I just want to be by myself.'

'No, you don't.' Patrick pulled her gently out of the car. 'Believe me, I've tried that in your situation. It doesn't work. Much better to have company when you're feeling down.'

'You're the wrong company. I need to yell and say bad things about your brother.'

'You can yell and say bad things about my brother. I promise not to defend him.' Patrick locked her car and pushed her towards the stable. 'We'll use your place. Mrs Thornton is staying the night so there's no guarantee of privacy in mine.'

Stella pulled the keys to the stable out of her pocket and promptly dropped them.

With a sigh, Patrick stooped and picked them up. 'Thank goodness you're not working in Resus tonight. I gather "Caring of Cumbria" wasn't what you were hoping for. Was he ugly?'

'I have no idea. He didn't turn up.' Stella pulled off her boots and dropped them by the door. 'Unfortunately, Daniel did.'

'Dan was at the pub?' Patrick closed the door behind them. 'I thought he had a date with the lawyer.'

'Well, apparently he found the time to come and ruin my evening first.' Stella filled the kettle, grateful for the cosy warmth of the stable. 'Patrick, it's really sweet of you to check up on me, but I'd like to be on my own.'

Ignoring her, Patrick slid onto one of the tall stools by the breakfast bar. 'So Daniel turned up—that's interesting.'

'It wasn't interesting.' Stella pulled a mug out of the cupboard. 'It was inconvenient, thoughtless, annoying—since you're determined not to let me have my tantrum on my own, do you want a coffee?'

'Please. Black, no sugar. I need the caffeine— I have a feeling I'm going to be back at the hospital soon.'

Stella made the coffee. 'You work too hard.'

'You sound like my ex-wife.' Patrick gave a wry smile and lifted his hand in a gesture of apology. 'Forget I said that—you're nothing like my ex-wife.'

'Do you hear from her?'

'No, and the only reason I care is for the kids. I can't believe she can just turn her back on her own children.' His tone was hard. 'Do you know what really gets to me? The fact that Alfie is OK about it. He saw so little of her that he's hardly noticed her absence.'

Stella handed him a mug. 'He's a sweet boy.'

'I just hope all of this hasn't put him off relationships. I worry that he'll think marriage isn't a good idea. Like Daniel.'

'Alfie doesn't seem to think that. It always amazes me how much children see. He's pretty wise for ten years old.' Stella passed him a packet of biscuits. 'I keep them for Alfie's visits. Please eat them or I'll eat them all myself. I'm in that sort of mood. Why did Daniel have to turn up at the pub tonight? Just bad luck, I suppose.'

Patrick took a biscuit. 'Bad luck doesn't take you to a pub when you have a date on the other side of town.'

'You don't think it was an accident that he was there?' Stella warmed her cold hands on her mug. 'How could he possibly have known where I was meeting the guy? Even you didn't know.'

'Actually, I did.' Patrick pulled a face. 'Alfie told me.'

Stella groaned. 'Alfie? You think he said something to Daniel?'

'I think he might have done. The two of them were talking earlier. Money changed hands. Sorry, Stella.'

'It isn't Alfie's fault. And to be honest, it wasn't even a secret. I suppose I didn't imagine for a moment Daniel would be interested. And even if he knew where I was going...' Stella put her mug down. 'Why would he bother coming? It doesn't make sense.'

'Doesn't it? If you want my opinion, I think my beloved twin couldn't face the thought of you seeing someone else. It isn't just me he doesn't want you to have a relationship with.' Patrick took a mouthful of coffee. 'It's anyone. What does that tell you?'

'That he's lost his mind,' Stella muttered, rubbing her forehead with her fingers as she tried to make sense of what he was saying. 'He didn't want me.'

'Oh, he wanted you, angel. And he obviously still wants you.'

Did he want her? Stella thought about the kiss and felt her cheeks turn pink. Quickly she picked up her coffee again. 'Even if the chemistry is still there, nothing has changed.' She was saying it to remind herself as much as Patrick. 'We want different things.'

'Yes. I know. That's what makes the whole thing complicated.' Patrick suppressed a yawn. 'So what did he say to you tonight?'

'He basically turned into a macho, chest-thumping, over-protective…' Stella ran out of adjectives. 'He didn't like the idea of me meeting a stranger.'

'Neither do I.'

'You didn't turn up and hang over me.'

'No, but I confess I did ring the landlord and ask him to watch out for you.' Patrick handed her his empty mug. 'I'd better go. I need to check that Alfie isn't watching unsuitable movies.'

'You rang the landlord?' Stella was stunned by that confession but Patrick simply smiled.

'Daniel isn't the only Buchannan brother who can be macho and over-protective.' He leaned forward and kissed her on the cheek. 'Goodnight. I'll leave you to your internet search. Next time make sure you pick someone who is going to show up.'

CHAPTER FIVE

'STELLA, have you seen Daniel?' Ellie hurried into the treatment room where Stella was just finishing a dressing. 'The paramedics are bringing in a baby with breathing problems. I need him.'

'I haven't seen him.' *She'd made sure she hadn't seen him.* She didn't want to set eyes on him until she'd calmed down.

The more she thought about what had happened the evening before, the angrier she became.

Stella saw her patient out of the room and Ellie looked at her closely.

'All right, tell me what's wrong. You've been hiding in the treatment room all morning.'

'I'm not hiding.'

'Your evening didn't go so well, did it? When you texted me to say you were at home, I gathered something was up. Was he creepy?'

'He didn't show up.' Neither had he emailed.

Stella frowned, finding it a little strange that he hadn't given her some reason for the fact that he hadn't shown up. Mind you, she hadn't given him her mobile number, had she? Apart from ringing through to the pub, he'd had no way of contacting her once she'd left the stable for the evening. But there had been no email waiting when she'd arrived home. 'Obviously he changed his mind.'

'So you just sat there for a bit and then left?'

Daniel's dark, handsome features swam in her brain. 'That's right. Early night.' And she felt horribly confused about the whole thing. Too confused even to talk to Ellie.

'You look tired for someone that had an early night.' Ellie leaned forward and gave her a hug. 'Why don't you come over to my house one evening this week? I can get the kids to sleep early and we can open a bottle and watch something romantic.'

'Romance isn't working for me at the moment, but thanks.' Stella hugged her back. 'You need to make the most of your evenings with Ben. You see little enough of him.'

'That's true, but there's something wonderfully soothing about talking to a girlfriend and ranting about the things that men just don't understand.' Ellie glanced at her watch. 'The ambulance will be here in a moment—I'd better go and find Daniel. I don't suppose I could persuade you to work in Paediatric Resus, could I?'

'What's happened to Andrea?'

'She had to transfer a patient to Theatre and she isn't back yet. And on top of that she irritates Daniel because she's slow.'

Knowing that to refuse would raise more questions than she wanted to answer, Stella gave a nod. 'All right. Tell me about this baby.'

'Five months old. Born at thirty-six weeks by Caesarean section—one of Patrick's, I think.' Ellie frowned. 'Anyway, the mum called the emergency services tonight after the baby turned blue and stopped breathing.' They hurried towards the paediatric area of the emergency department and met Daniel heading in the same direction.

It was the first time Stella had seen him since the previous evening—since the kiss—and she felt the colour flare in her cheeks. Despite her best intentions, all she could think about was the way his mouth had felt against hers.

His eyes raked her face, held hers for a disturbing moment and then his jaw tightened and he pushed open the doors to Resus with slightly more force than was necessary. 'What have we got?'

A mess, Stella thought helplessly, thinking of their own situation.

'Five-month-old baby…' Ellie repeated the information she'd given Stella, just as the paramedics arrived with the baby.

A pale-faced woman with no make-up and untidy hair was with them, holding a squirming toddler by the hand. 'Please don't make me go and sit in the waiting room. I can't bear to leave Poppy.'

'You're her mother?' Daniel walked across to the trolley and the woman nodded.

'We've been up all night for three nights and I can't even think straight any more.' Her eyes filled. 'She stopped breathing.' She broke off as the toddler started to whine and Stella took one look at his exhausted, stressed mother and scooped him up.

'Come and see what's in my magic box,' she whispered into his ear, and the toddler stopped grizzling and looked interested. Stella pulled out the toy box that was hidden away for occasions such as this, and settled the toddler on the floor. 'This is full of exciting things. See if you can find my special blue car. I'm just going to see to your sister. I'll be back in a minute.'

While Daniel was questioning the mother, Stella attached the baby to a cardiac monitor and a pulse oximeter.

'Sats are 92 in air,' she murmured, and Daniel glanced at the monitor.

'Let's give her humidified oxygen and ask the paediatric registrar to come down. Whatever the outcome of my examination, she's going to need to be admitted.' Removing a stethoscope from his pocket, he turned back to the mother. 'You say that you've been up all night for three nights. Was that when she first became ill?'

'I thought she just had a cold. She just had a runny nose and a bit of a temperature. It's that time of year, isn't it? And then suddenly she started coughing—this horrible dry cough. And she stopped feeding.'

'A baby with a respiratory infection can't always take the same amount of food as usual.' Daniel slid the jumper over the baby's head and undid the vest. 'So what happened to make you call the ambulance?'

'I put her down for a nap and when I looked at her she was blue and she stopped breathing for a bit. Honestly, I didn't imagine it.'

'Her respirations are 70,' Stella said, and Daniel gave a nod as he shifted the vest and looked at the baby's chest.

'I'm sure you didn't imagine it.' He glanced at the mother with a smile, everything about him calm and reassuring. 'It isn't uncommon for young babies with bronchiolitis to have pauses in their breathing and I suspect that's what's going on here. I'm going to take a good look at her and then we'll decide how best to treat her.'

'I honestly thought she was going to die.'

'There's nothing more frightening than being on your own at home with a sick baby. It's hard to think straight, especially when you've been up all night.' Daniel watched the baby's chest rise and fall. 'You did the right thing to bring her in. We have an excellent paediatric department here and we won't be sending Poppy home until we're happy with her.'

In response to his sympathetic comments, the

mother put her hand to her face and started to cry. 'Sorry—you must think I'm a total nutcase, it's just that I'm *so* tired and I've been so worried.'

'I'm not surprised. Any normal parent would be out of their mind with worry.' Daniel gestured to the chair and then put the stethoscope in his ears. 'Sit down before you drop and I have to treat you, too. Once I have a better idea what's going on, you can get yourself a hot drink in the café down the corridor. You look as though you need one.' Then he turned back to the baby, his hands infinitely gentle as he examined her.

'Poppy sick?' The toddler wandered across to the trolley, clutching a blue car, and Stella admired the toy before turning back to help Daniel.

He was so good with children and that made the whole thing so much worse.

Although she knew he didn't think so himself, Stella knew that Daniel would make a wonderful father.

While he concentrated on his tiny patient, she found herself looking at him. Why couldn't she be indifferent? He was *so* unsuitable. He didn't want what she wanted. So why did she still find him so desperately attractive? She gazed at the strong, bold lines of his bone structure and the dark shadow that emphasised his jaw. And her heart stumbled.

Daniel removed the stethoscope from his ears and met her gaze. He frowned briefly, clearly aware that she was thinking about more than the patient. 'Fine inspiratory crackles,' he said gruffly, 'and she has a high-pitched expiratory wheeze. She has nasal flaring, grunting and her chest is visibly hyper-inflated so I think we're looking at a diagnosis of bronchiolitis. Did you ring Paeds?'

Stella pulled herself together. 'Yes. The registrar is just finishing a lumbar puncture and then he'll be down.' She turned her attention back to the baby, telling herself that her relationship with Daniel would become easier over time. It was bound to feel hard at first, wasn't it? It was up to her to move on.

Maybe 'Caring of Cumbria' hadn't worked out—but that didn't mean she wouldn't meet someone else. She wasn't going to give up at the first fence.

'What exactly is bronchiolitis?' The exhausted young mother stood up and stroked her baby's head gently. 'Could I have avoided it somehow?'

'It's a viral infection of the small airway, very common in the winter months, especially in this age group.' Daniel took his pen out of his pocket. 'There's absolutely nothing you could have done.'

'I feel like a terrible mother. I feel like I've let her down. I should have brought her days ago.'

'She wasn't as ill as this days ago, or you would have brought her.' Daniel wrote up some drugs on the notes. 'You haven't let her down. You've done all the right things. You're a brilliant mum.'

The woman flushed. 'I don't feel brilliant. I feel...incoherent. I haven't been to bed for three nights.'

'That's why you're brilliant,' Daniel said easily. 'Some mothers would have just gone back to sleep. You've put yourself through the wringer because you've been watching over your child. That makes you brilliant in my book. How many feeds has Poppy had today in comparison to normal?'

The mother flushed but it was obvious that Daniel's words had bolstered her self-confidence and given her the extra strength she needed to get through the crisis.

Stella studied Daniel's profile, wondering what

his own mother had been like. She knew that his childhood had been far from idyllic, but he rarely divulged any details.

He had firm views on mothers, she knew that. And fathers.

And he didn't think he'd make a good one.

Oblivious to her scrutiny, he was scribbling on the notes. 'How many wet nappies?'

The mother pulled a face. 'I—I don't know. Why is that important?'

'Because it helps us assess how dehydrated she is. We may need to give her some fluid into her vein, but I'm going to leave that to my paediatric colleagues to decide.'

'Can you give her antibiotics or something?'

'It's caused by a virus so antibiotics won't help.' Daniel looked up as the door opened. 'This is Deborah—she's the paediatric doctor.' He outlined the case to Deborah, who immediately arranged for the child to be admitted.

Stella watched the easy smile he gave to the other doctor and wondered whether they'd had a relationship in the past two years.

Gritting her teeth, she gathered up the baby's things. *None of her business,* she reminded herself. She no longer had any interest in Daniel Buchannan's love life.

And that was the way it was going to stay.

As the paediatric team took over care of the baby and transferred her, she expected Daniel to go back to work. Instead, he closed the door of Resus so that the two of them were alone.

'Listen, about last night—'

'Yes, last night.' Her temper exploded, fuelled by all the confusing feelings he'd released inside her. 'Don't you *ever* kiss me again, Daniel Buchannan. Do you hear me?'

'You kissed me, too.'

'Yes, I did. And it was a mistake!' She glared at him. 'I didn't come back here to get involved with you again. What do you think I am? Stupid? Some sort of masochist? You think I want to put myself through that pain again?'

His eyes narrowed. 'Stella—'

'Kiss me again and I'll injure you!' She stabbed her finger towards him. 'If you want a woman, I'm sure your lawyer will oblige.'

His expression was defensive. 'You have no reason to be jealous of her.'

'I'm not jealous. I'm angry. I'm angry that you

can be so—so…' She stumbled over the words. '*Careless* about my feelings.'

'I'm not careless,' Daniel said roughly. 'It's because I care that I broke off our engagement. I knew I couldn't give you what you wanted. I couldn't be what you wanted me to be. If I'd married you, I would have made you miserable.'

'Well, breaking off our engagement didn't exactly make my day, either!' Furious with herself and with him, Stella turned away and started clearing up the equipment from the trolley with more clatter and energy than was entirely necessary. 'We can work together, Daniel, because we're both professionals. As for the rest of it—I want you to stay away from me.' *Because she didn't trust herself…*

With a soft curse, Daniel strode towards her, his eyes glittering dangerously as he moved her away from the trolley and backed her against the wall. 'Enough of this,' he growled, planting his arms either side of her so that she was trapped. 'Are you trying to pretend you don't feel anything?'

'No, I'm not. But I don't *want* to feel anything, can't you understand that?' Her legs were shaking and her insides were as hot and fluid as molten lava. 'You *hurt* me, Daniel.'

'You think I don't know that?' He put his hand under her chin and forced her to look at him. 'You think I don't know exactly what I did two years ago? Believe me, I know.'

'So why did you kiss me again?' She tried to ignore his tantalising male scent and those blue eyes, programmed to drive a woman wild. 'You want to put me through it all a second time?'

'No.' His gaze dropped to her mouth and lingered there. 'I kissed you because I can't be that close to you and not want to kiss you. That's how it's always been. Most of the time I manage to control it but last night—last night, I didn't. I was angry that you were meeting a stranger. Angry that you wore the red dress.' The expression in his eyes was personal—*intimate*—and Stella felt the breath jam in her throat.

'What I wear isn't any of your business.' His face was close to hers, just a breath away from touching.

'Why did you come back, Stella?'

She gave a low moan and closed her eyes, struggling against instincts that were stronger than her. 'I've told you why. Because this is my home.' Her heart was thumping dangerously hard and her body yearned to melt into his. 'Are you suggesting this is all my fault?' *Oh, God, of course it was her fault. She'd overestimated the strength of her willpower, hadn't she?*

'You knew I was here, but you chose to come back. You knew what would happen when we were alone together. Look at me.' His fingers tightened on her chin, demanding—*possessive*. 'Admit it, Stella. This was always going to be difficult.'

She looked at him and immediately wished she hadn't because eye contact simply intensified the chemistry. 'Why would it be difficult?! You didn't want me—'

'That isn't true. You know that isn't true.' His mouth was dangerously close to hers. 'I won't make a good husband or a good father, but that deficiency in my make-up has no effect on my skills as a lover.'

A delicious shiver ran through her body. 'Dan, please—'

'I've always wanted you,' he breathed huskily. 'I've wanted you from the very first day I saw you.'

'Stop it!' Stella twisted her head away, trying to free herself from temptation. '*You're* the one making this difficult.'

'No. It's difficult because our relationship didn't really end. I told you that I didn't want marriage and children, but I never once told you that I didn't want you.'

Stella pushed at his chest and struggled to find willpower. 'You wanted sex with no commitment.'

'I made a commitment,' he said roughly. 'I was with you. There was no one else for me.'

Thinking about their relationship was bitter-sweet. She'd been so excited about the future, in love for the first time in her life…

'It wasn't enough, Daniel. I want more than that. I'm old-fashioned. I want a man to love me enough to marry me.' Her voice broke because it seemed impossible to imagine ever loving a man as much as she loved Daniel. 'Why are we going over this again? Leave me alone, Daniel. I'm trying to build a new life.'

'Is that why you're meeting strange men in pubs? Is that the "new life" you want?' The sudden hardness of his tone slashed like the blade of a knife and her chin lifted.

'That's none of your business.'

'I'm just worried about you, that's all.'

'You don't need to worry. I'm not your problem Daniel.' Unsettled by her own feelings as much as the look in his eyes, Stella ducked under his arm and walked towards the door, her legs shaking so badly she could hardly walk. 'Neither am I your responsibility. If I choose to meet a stranger in a pub, that's my decision.'

'It's a lousy decision.' His blue eyes glittered dangerously as he watched her retreat. 'Why are you meeting men over the internet?'

'Why not?' She held his gaze and for a moment they just looked at each other.

'It isn't safe to meet strangers,' he said roughly. 'You could get hurt.'

'*You* hurt me, Daniel. *You hurt me.*' Stella turned away, confused and frustrated. Was he asking her not to meet anyone? Was he suggesting that they resurrect their relationship? Part of her was appalled at the thought, but another tiny part of her was desperately hopeful and she *hated* the fact that she could still feel that way.

'I know I hurt you.' His voice was low and impossibly sexy. 'I know I can't be what you want me to be.' He broke off and muttered something under his breath, his shoulders visibly tense. 'Just be careful, that's all I ask. If you want to meet a man, go to the Christmas party. At least it's a safe environment. You know lots of the people and you're less likely to get hurt.'

Her fantasies shattered like glass on concrete.

He was encouraging her to meet someone else.

'You can just as easily get hurt by the people you love as by strangers,' Stella said pointedly, turning and looking him in the eye. 'And when I need your help or advice to meet a man, I'll ask.' Without giving him time to reply, she stalked out of the room and let the door swing shut behind her, wishing for the first time in her life that she'd never met Daniel Buchannan.

Stretched out in a chair in his office, exhausted after eleven hours with no break, Daniel stared blankly at the computer screen, his mind full of the night before.

He never should have kissed her.

What had possessed him to do such an utterly stupid thing?

As if things hadn't been hard enough *before* that.

He still didn't understand exactly why he'd lost control.

One moment he'd been furiously angry, the next he'd been kissing her. Usually with women he choreographed every move—he was *always* in control. He made sure of it. He knew when he was going to ask them out, he knew where he was going to take them—control was part of the way he protected himself.

Only with Stella there was no control. And there never had been.

Sliding his hand over his face, he muttered a black oath.

Nothing had changed between them. Except that they were no longer together.

Dwelling on that uncomfortable truth, Daniel glanced up to see his brother standing in the doorway. 'What are you doing here? Is someone giving birth in my department?'

'No. I have some news. And I need a favour.' Patrick frowned at him. 'You look as though you're in a filthy mood. What's wrong?'

'Nothing.' Somehow Daniel couldn't bring himself to confess his thoughts about Stella.

He waited while his brother sprawled in the only armchair in his office. 'You don't look so good yourself.'

'Tired.' Patrick closed his eyes and Daniel frowned slightly.

'Is it the job or the kids?' Out of the corner of his eye, Daniel surveyed his desk, barely visible beneath the piles of files and papers that people wanted him to read. For a brief moment he wondered what would happen if he just tipped the lot into the bin. Would anyone notice? He didn't have time to deal with any of it all anyway, so it may as well be in the bin. His computer was telling him that he had seventy-two new messages in his inbox and he stifled the temptation to just switch the thing off at the mains. 'What's the problem?' *Apart from the fact your wife left you with two little kids.*

'I'm knackered.' His brother opened his eyes briefly. 'If the labour ward rings, you haven't seen me.'

'That bad, huh?' Daniel gave a sympathetic grin and transferred the files on his desk to the floor. 'Busy night?'

'Not particularly.' His brother's eyes drifted

shut again. 'But I didn't get any sleep, thanks to a certain woman in my life.'

Daniel gave a slow smile of masculine approval. 'Now, that *is* good news. I've been telling you for months that it's time for you to get out there again. Tell me that she was incredible in bed, cooks like an angel and is dying to take on a single dad with two small children who spends most of his waking hours working.'

Patrick opened his eyes. 'What are you talking about?'

'The woman you spent last night with—I want the details. Blonde? Brunette? Redhead? God, I love redheads. My lawyer is a redhead.'

'You always preferred blondes.'

'Well, now I prefer redheads. Very dominant and assertive.' Omitting to mention that he couldn't help comparing every blonde to Stella, Daniel noticed more emails fly into his inbox and swivelled the chair so that he could no longer see the screen. 'And we were talking about you, not me. Why don't we grab a beer after work and you can give me the details?'

'Can't. I need to get home. And there isn't a woman. At least, not the sort that you mean.'

Patrick ran a hand over his face. 'It was Posy who kept me awake. I was talking about Posy.'

The smile left Daniel's face. 'You're exhausted because of your three-year-old daughter?'

'That's right.' Patrick's eyes closed again and his head dropped back against the chair. 'I don't know whether she's teething or whether she has a cold coming but she's really fractious at the moment. In the end she slept in my bed and it was hell. She always lies horizontally so her feet are in my—'

'You know what?' Daniel lifted a hand as he interrupted him. 'This is too much detail. I honestly don't need to know about the sleeping patterns of a three-year-old.'

Patrick was silent for a moment and then he opened his eyes and looked straight at his brother. 'You're very fond of Posy. And of Alfie.'

'Of course I am.' Daniel waved a hand. 'I'm a doting uncle. The job description for doting uncle is that I smother them with extravagant gifts on various important dates like birthdays and Christmas and as they grow up I take them on the odd climbing expedition and for rides in my fast sports car to impress their friends.'

Patrick was silent for a moment and it seemed to Daniel that his twin brother looked more exhausted than he'd ever seen him.

'You need some time away.'

Patrick gave a nod. 'That's what I'm planning.'

'You are? Without the kids? Perfect. What's the plan?'

'Do you remember that lecture I gave in Chicago? Well, they've offered me a job. Part clinical–part academic. It would give me more time at home with the kids—'

'A job in Chicago?' Daniel frowned slightly, unsure how he felt about his brother relocating to the States. 'You're considering that?'

'I thought it was worth a look. They want me to come across and meet them. Look around, interview…' Patrick shrugged. 'You know the score.'

'Great. Go for it. Fresh start. Well, at least go and talk to them.'

'I'd like to. And that brings me to the favour I need.'

'Of course. I know your sweet ex-wife cost you a fortune. I don't know how you've coped.' Even when Patrick's petulant, moody wife had finally stopped having tantrums and left him *and* the children, his brother had just gritted his teeth and got on with his life. He'd shifted his workload so that he could continue in his role as obs and gynae consultant and still spend time at home with the children. Daniel reached for his chequebook. 'How much?'

'I don't need money. Money isn't my problem. I need a different sort of favour.'

'Name it.' Daniel thought of the hell that his brother had been through since his wife had left and waved a hand expressively. 'Anything. What do you need? A lift to the airport?'

'I need you to look after the kids.'

'What?' Daniel stared at him with undisguised horror. 'You have to be kidding. No. Absolutely no.'

'You said anything.'

'Anything *but that*.' Daniel launched himself out of his chair, knocking pens and papers onto the floor. 'Why would you even ask me that? I'm the last person in the world that any sane person would want looking after their kids. I'm terrible with kids. That's why I don't have any of my own.'

'You're my family. And you're their family.'

'That's no reason to punish them! Or me.'

Daniel felt panic mingle with guilt. 'Don't ask me to do this, Ric.'

'I'm asking. And it isn't a punishment for the kids. They love you. You've been a constant in their lives since they were born.'

Nervous now, Daniel paced around his office. 'From a distance. I told you, I do the fun stuff. I don't do any of the nitty-gritty practical stuff. I wouldn't know how. What if they can't sleep, or they fall over—well, actually the falling over bit would be about the only thing I'd be qualified to deal with, but...' Daniel felt the prickle of sweat on his brow and ran a hand over his face. 'Can't you just take them with you?'

'Posy is too little and I don't want Alfie to miss school. And who would look after them while I'm looking around the hospital and talking to people? I don't want some stranger caring for my kids. You'll be fine. It's another week until the Christmas holidays start.'

'Why can't Mrs Thornton do it?'

'I can't give her sole responsibility for the children.'

'Stella?'

'I can't ask her to look after two kids that aren't hers.'

'You're asking me—'

'Because you're my brother.' Patrick sank his hands into his hair. 'Do you honestly think I'd be asking you if I had a choice? I know you'll hate every minute, but I also know the kids will be safe with you.'

Daniel's heart was pounding. 'Ask me anything else,' he said hoarsely. 'A horse for Posy. Anything. But don't ask me to look after them.'

'Posy is too young to need a horse.'

'See?' Daniel spread his hands. 'I don't even know that. I don't know what children do at what age. I wouldn't be safe with them. You're mad even to ask me.'

'You won't have to do much,' Patrick said wearily. 'Just give them breakfast and get Alfie to school. Then you bring Posy here and drop her into the hospital crèche on your way to work.'

'I can't fit the kids in my sports car.'

'We'll swap cars. I'll take the Porsche and you can use my four-wheel drive.'

Daniel lifted an eyebrow. 'If that's supposed to be an incentive, you don't know me very well,' he drawled. 'Listen. I'm the last person in the world that anyone would want looking after their kids. I don't know anything about kids.'

'You work in A and E. You know a great deal about kids.'

'I know how to fix them when they're broken!' Daniel glared at him. 'And I'm assuming you don't want yours broken, which they will be if I look after them!' He felt something close to panic rise inside him and then he looked at his brother—saw the dark shadows in his eyes.

'You're my brother,' Patrick said softly. 'That makes you suitable. You're the only person I trust.'

Daniel lifted his hand to his throat, feeling as though he was being strangled. 'All right, I'll do it.' His mouth was moving even while his brain was still trying to refuse. 'But you have to leave me some textbooks or something.'

'They're just kids, Dan,' Patrick looked amused. 'You don't need books. They'll tell you what they want.'

'Posy is so little. How am I going to know what she wants?'

'She'll tell you. Alfie is good with her. He'll

help.' Patrick glanced at the clock. 'I'd better get back. Thanks. And stop worrying. It's only for four days, Dan. What can possibly go wrong?'

'I assume you don't want me to answer that.' Daniel strode back to his desk and delved under a pile of papers for his mobile. 'The first thing I'm doing is calling Andrea.'

'Your frosty lawyer? How's that going?'

'We've both been too busy for me to thaw her out,' Daniel muttered. 'One of the disadvantages of dating a career-woman is that they're too involved in their career to see you. And when she's available, I'm not. This place is death on a relationship, you know that.' Seeing his brother's face, he closed his eyes briefly. 'Sorry.'

'It's all right. Carly didn't leave because of the job—that was just her excuse. She left because she was Carly.' Patrick rose to his feet. 'Why would you call Andrea?'

'Because she's a woman. She'll know what to do with a ten-year-old and a three-year-old.'

'I wouldn't be too sure about that.'

'Well, she's going to know more than me.' Daniel dialled the number. 'When are you leaving?'

'Saturday.'

'That gives me four days to bring in reinforcements.'

'If you get stuck, you can always bang on the stable door and ask Stella to help. The kids love her.'

Daniel thought about the kiss and gritted his teeth. Stella had made it clear she didn't want him anywhere near her, and he was in agreement.

If last night had taught him anything, it was that the chemistry between them was still alive and well. And that could only lead to trouble.

No way would he be banging on the stable door.

CHAPTER SIX

IT SNOWED for the next four days and they were so busy in the emergency department that when she finally had a day off, Stella slept late.

Relishing the thought of a whole weekend ahead of her, she decided to check whether Patrick needed any help preparing for his trip.

Dressing in warm clothes, she picked her way gingerly across the snow-covered yard and banged on the door.

Daniel yanked it open. One of the kittens shot past him and out of the door and Stella stooped and caught it. She was so shocked to see Daniel there that she was glad of a reason to hide her scarlet face.

'Where do you think you're going?' She cuddled the kitten close and then looked at Daniel, trying to keep her expression neutral. 'I didn't know you were here. I was going to talk to Patrick…' Her voice tailed off as she saw the red streak on his cheek. 'What happened to you? Are you bleeding?'

Daniel lifted a hand and scrubbed at the mark. 'It's probably paint. Posy is painting. She doesn't appear to have a very good sense of direction with the brush. Thanks for catching the kitten. I keep forgetting I'm not supposed to open the door.'

'Right.' The situation felt horribly awkward. 'Is Patrick around?'

'He's gone into town to get a few things for his trip. I'm having a practice run with the children.'

Stella looked at the paint on his cheek. 'And how's that going?'

'Both kids were still alive last time I looked.' His lazy drawl was a contrast to the tension she saw in his eyes.

'You'll be fine.' Stella's eye caught movement behind him. 'That red paint you mentioned— Posy appears to be painting on the wall. Is that what you had planned?'

Daniel turned swiftly, growled deep in his throat and made a dive for Posy. 'How did she get there? I left her safely occupied at the table.'

'Three-year-olds don't always stay where you

put them.' It was impossible not to laugh. 'How are your decorating skills?'

'About the same as my childminding skills.' Daniel prised the paintbrush out of Posy's chubby hand. 'On the paper, Posy, not on the wall. The *paper.*'

Posy's lip wobbled and Daniel scooped her up in his arms. 'Don't cry. No one cries on my shift. Understand?'

In response to that rough command, Posy plopped her head on his shoulder, her blonde curls a stark contrast to Daniel's dark masculinity. As the child curled her arm round his neck, Stella saw his mouth tighten and a muscle work in his lean, hard jaw. But his hand came up to steady her and he rubbed the child's back awkwardly.

'I don't deserve that cuddle,' he said gruffly, and Stella suddenly found it impossible to swallow. Emotion stung her eyes and pricked at her throat and she found herself thinking things she didn't want to be thinking.

Her thoughts were already dominated by Daniel the doctor and Daniel the lover—the last thing she needed was to be thinking of Daniel the father.

He didn't want to be a father, she reminded herself. *He didn't want that.*

The fact that little Posy was clinging to him adoringly didn't change anything.

'I'll try and catch Patrick later.' Her mind in turmoil, she backed away, still holding the kitten. 'I just wanted to wish him luck. What time is his flight?'

'He leaves for the airport just after lunch.'

'Stella!' Alfie walked across the yard, another two kittens in his arms. 'Is Daddy back yet?' His voice had a distinct wobble in it and Stella dropped into a crouch next to him.

'What's wrong?'

'Mary and Joseph escaped. I'm worried they've caught a cold.'

Stella stooped and examined the kittens. 'They seem happy enough.'

'They've been outside in the snow.'

'Well, take them back into the house and we'll watch them.'

'Why does Dad have to go?' Alfie looked miserable. 'What if the kittens are poorly when he's gone?'

'Then I'll fix it,' Daniel said firmly, still holding Posy.

Alfie looked at him doubtfully. 'You don't know anything about kids or kittens. I heard you telling Dad.'

'Well, I…' Daniel cleared his throat, 'I don't know much, that's true, but I'm learning fast. In the last five minutes I've learned not to turn my back on Posy when she has a paintbrush in her hand.'

'I could have told you that.' Alfie looked at his sister. 'And you can't turn your back on her in the bath because she likes to splash all the water onto the floor.'

'I'm expected to bath you?' Daniel's handsome face lost some of its colour. 'That sounds complicated. Maybe we could skip that bit.'

Alfie held the kittens against his chest. 'Dad's away for four days. We'll be smelly.'

'Smelly, but in one piece,' Daniel muttered under his breath. 'All right. Fine. I can lead a trauma team. I'm sure I can manage to bath two kids.'

'I can bath myself. It's just Posy that needs help.'

'That's what's worrying me.' But his hand was still stroking Posy's back and his eyes were fixed on Alfie's face. 'How am I doing so far? Have I forgotten anything? Done anything wrong?'

'You're doing OK. For a beginner. You didn't cook the pasta for long enough but I don't mind it chewy.' Alfie shrugged, but his eyes were just a little too bright. 'Is Dad going to say goodbye before he goes?'

'Of course he is.' Daniel watched his nephew. 'Are you worried about him going?'

'No. I'm not a baby.' Alfie's tone was fierce. 'It just feels a bit—weird, him leaving this close to Christmas. There's stuff we should be doing. Stuff he should be here for.'

'Stuff.' Daniel looked out of his depth and cast a helpless glance at Stella. 'What stuff?'

'Christmas stuff.' Alfie held onto the wriggling kittens. 'Don't worry about it. You don't have to do it. I know you didn't do much at Christmas when you were kids. Dad told me it was always a pretty rough time for you.'

Stella hid her surprise. She knew that Daniel's childhood hadn't been happy, but she hadn't known that Christmas had been particularly bad.

The sudden tension in Daniel's shoulders made Stella want to question exactly what

Daniel's Christmases had been like as a child. In all the time they'd been together, he had never mentioned Christmas to her. In fact, he'd said very little about his childhood, except to intimate that his parents' relationship had been grim. Whenever she'd tried to probe, he'd changed the subject.

'This "stuff" you're talking about...' Daniel held Posy close '...we can do some of that while your dad is away, if you want to. You just have to tell me what you want to do.'

'You mean that?' Alfie's face brightened. 'Can we go and buy the tree? Dad was going to take us to the forest this afternoon but then he didn't have enough time and he said it would have to wait.'

Daniel nodded. 'We can go and get a tree.' He gave Stella a faint smile. 'Might be easier to be outdoors than indoors with these two.'

'Don't you believe it,' she murmured under her breath, but Alfie was already fizzing with excitement.

'The forest will be so cool after all that snow. Can Stella come with us?'

Daniel looked at Stella and she knew he was thinking the same thing that she was thinking.

That neither of them wanted to go on a trip together. And neither of them wanted to disappoint Alfie.

Daniel gave a lopsided smile. 'Will you come?'

She ought to say no. After what had happened between them this week, they needed to spend as little time together as possible.

'Pleeease,' Alfie begged, his eyes wide with hope and his arms full of kittens. 'Please come, Stella. It won't be any fun if you don't come.'

'How can I say no?' Stella gave a weak smile and the tiny kitten she was holding climbed up her jumper and rubbed itself against her face. 'It sounds like fun.' If one's definition of fun was spending an afternoon doing something guaranteed to cause significant mental anguish.

'Great. Then you can spend the rest of the day with us and help us decorate it.' Alfie was looking much more cheerful. 'We can toast marshmallows and watch a Christmas movie on the television, like we did two Christmases ago.'

Two Christmases ago when her heart had been breaking and she'd cuddled Alfie, wondering why she'd had to choose between the man she wanted and the family she longed for.

Stella swallowed. Could she spend the day with Daniel? She felt as though someone was tying ropes around her, preventing her escaping from a situation that was becoming more and more difficult. 'We'll see.'

'Don't say "We'll see". That always means "No".' Alfie looked at her pleadingly. 'Promise you'll come and help us decorate it afterwards.'

Stella's mouth moved without any intervention from her brain. 'I promise.'

'Great.' Bouncing with excitement, Alfie turned back to the house. 'I'll just put Mary and Joseph inside, then I'll take Gabriel from you.'

Stella looked down at the kitten in her arms. 'This is Gabriel?'

'Yes. You can tell because of the black splodge on his ear.' Alfie darted inside the house and Stella was suddenly painfully conscious of Daniel watching her.

Perhaps she should have said no. She should have made some excuse. Choosing a Christmas tree with Daniel and two gorgeous children was going to be something close to torture.

But it was illogical to think about what might have been when she knew it never would have been. That was why they'd parted, wasn't it? Because they both wanted different things.

He was looking after Patrick's children because he was fiercely loyal to his brother, not because he had a secret wish to be a father.

'Sorry.' His tone was rough and apologetic. 'I didn't intend you to be roped into helping.'

'I love the children.' The conversation was stilted. Polite and formal. They were behaving like strangers, not two people who had been lovers. *Two people who had shared everything.*

'I thought if I took them to buy a tree, it might take their minds off their dad leaving. And I think I'm probably better at doing outdoor stuff than indoor stuff.' Daniel gave a rueful glance at the red marks on the wall and Stella smiled.

'That will come off with a good scrub. And I think it's a great idea to take them to the forest to get the tree. Once you've decorated the house, they'll be too excited about Christmas to think too much about Patrick. Christmas routines always do that.' She saw something flicker in his eyes and remembered what Alfie had said about Daniel's experience of Christmas.

But she had no idea what that was, and she had

no opportunity to ask because Alfie reappeared and Patrick pulled up in the car.

Stella hugged him, wished him luck on his trip and then retreated to the stable to dress in something suitable for an excursion to the forest in winter.

Part of her wanted to back out of the trip, but she knew that if she did that Alfie would be disappointed and she didn't want that to happen. She'd chosen to come back, she reminded herself. Patrick and the children were part of her life and Daniel was a part of *their* lives. If the only way she could cope with not being with him was to avoid him, she wasn't doing very well, was she?

The forest was like a winter playground and the children soon forgot about Patrick's absence, enchanted by the volume of snow.

'We haven't had snow like this for years. No, Posy—don't take your boots off.' Daniel bent down and scooped her up, shaking his head in frustration. 'You can't walk in the snow in bare feet.'

'You remembered boots and a coat.' Stella retrieved the boots. 'I'm impressed.'

'Posy hates her boots,' Alfie told them, scooping snow into a ball. Then he gave an impish smile and lobbed the snow straight at Daniel.

Shaking snow out of his hair, Daniel carefully handed a startled Posy to Stella and then turned on his nephew. Alfie gave a squeal of delighted anticipation and sprinted up the snowy path, slipping and sliding until Daniel caught up with him. They both tumbled in the snow, rolling and play-fighting until both of them were covered in clumps of freezing white powder.

'Me, too.' Posy wriggled in her arms and Stella deftly slid the child's feet back into her boots and let her run towards the others.

For a moment Stella just stood still, enjoying the peace of her surroundings. The air was crisp and cold and she could smell wood smoke.

It was a perfect winter day.

A couple walked passed her, smiling towards Daniel and Alfie who were still rolling. 'That's how a father is supposed to behave.' The woman laughed and Stella managed a smile.

'Yes.' She wondered what Daniel would say if he'd heard that comment.

That the last thing in the world he wanted was commitment and the responsibility of children.

But he was taking his responsibility seriously, wasn't he?

Correctly assuming that the children would be unsettled by their father leaving, he'd immediately arranged a trip.

Stella watched, suddenly confused. It wasn't that he didn't love the children, because he did. And it wasn't that he wasn't good with them, because he was.

He didn't feel he'd be a good father. But why?

'You're looking very serious.' Daniel was standing in front of her and she hadn't even noticed. She was about to reply when she saw the wicked gleam in his eyes and then gasped as he lifted a huge lump of snow and stuffed it down the neck of her jumper.

'Oh! You...' Gasping at the sudden cold and trying to shake the snow out of her jumper, Stella shot him a warning glare. 'I'll get my own back.'

'I can't wait.' He spread his arms wide, inviting her retaliation, and Stella gave him a slow smile.

'It's going to come when you least expect it.'

'Sweetheart, I'm shivering with terror.' He was teasing her now and the combination of laughing blue eyes and rough, dark jaw made him impossibly sexy.

'You will be shivering, Daniel,' Stella promised, shaking the last of the snow from the inside of her jumper and trying to subdue the shivers in her own body. *Shivers that had nothing to do with the cold.* 'Trust me. By the time I've finished, you'll be shivering.'

Alfie danced on the spot, laughing and jumping to keep warm. 'Can we go and choose our tree now?'

They walked along the path until they reached the clearing. A fire was burning in the centre and trees of various sizes had been piled together.

'This one?' Daniel strode up to the nearest tree but Alfie looked horrified.

'Too small.' He sprinted to the far end of the clearing and waved his arms madly. 'This one.'

Daniel heaved it upright and stared at the top in disbelief. 'This tree will never fit indoors.'

'It's perfect.' Alfie caught his arm. 'Can we have it, Uncle Daniel? *Pleeease?*'

Stella watched with amusement as Daniel

made a valiant effort to resist Alfie's superior persuasive technique.

'Alfie, this is just too large for your house. It's—'

'If I can have this tree I'll be so good,' Alfie coaxed. His cheeks were pink with the cold and he was so excited he could barely stand still. 'I'll go to bed when you say, I'll help with Posy and if you make any mistakes I won't tell Dad.'

'Done. That's an offer too good to turn down.' A smile in his eyes, Daniel dug his wallet out of his pocket. 'Where do I pay?'

'That man over there—but you have to carry the tree to the car.'

'But that's miles away. Don't they deliver? I don't suppose my brother wants his four-wheel drive full of pine needles.'

'That's the best bit,' Alfie said happily. 'The car smells like Christmas for months. Dad is always complaining.'

'In that case, let's go for it. Anything that winds my brother up is fine by me. And if I discover that he put a dent in my Porsche on the way to the airport, I'll volunteer to transport everyone's Christmas trees in his vehicle.'

Alfie giggled. 'Dad would go demented.'

'That's the general idea.' Daniel blew on his hands to warm them. 'Come on, let's get this tree home before we all freeze.'

How had he managed to land the job of decorating the house for Christmas?

What did he know about a family Christmas? Nothing.

Daniel manoeuvred the tree through the front door of Patrick's barn and shifted it upright in the corner of the huge living room. 'Here?'

He looked at the excitement in both the children's faces and felt something shift inside him.

He'd blocked out almost all his memories of childhood Christmases, but he was entirely sure that his face had never looked as bright and happy as Alfie's.

Christmas had been a battlefield, with carnage strewn where there should have been presents and goodwill.

'Uncle Daniel? You're looking all funny.' Alfie peered at him through the folds of his brightly coloured scarf. 'Are you OK?'

'I'm OK.' Daniel cleared his throat and pushed

his way through the black thoughts that rolled across his brain like menacing stormclouds. 'Let's get this tree sorted out. Is this a good place for it?'

Alfie dropped the scarf on the floor and nodded his approval. 'It looks good.'

'It looks *big.*' Stella was laughing as she removed Posy's hat and coat and Daniel glanced towards her and found he couldn't look away. Her blonde hair slid in a smooth, shiny sheet over her coat and her cheeks were flushed from the cold. He looked at her lips and knew that if he kissed them now, they'd be cold. And he also knew they wouldn't stay cold for long. The heat the two of them managed to generate would melt the polar icecap.

Her gaze met his and he saw her smile falter as her thoughts slid in the same direction as his.

'Dad got the decorations out for us.' Alfie dragged a huge box across the room. 'You have to do the lights first. Stella? You're not concentrating!' His excitement was infectious and Stella turned back to him, her cheeks even pinker than they'd been a few moments earlier.

'I hope these lights work.' She helped him unravel the lights, chatting easily about what he'd been doing at school and his part in the nativity play. Posy was popping bubble wrap and giggling with delight.

Daniel had a strange feeling of detachment— as if he were watching them from the other side of a pane of glass.

Was this how Christmas was supposed to feel?

Aware that Stella was looking at him, he forced a smile. 'Are all those bulbs working?'

'Yes.' Stella stood up. Her cheerful red skirt had ridden up her thighs, exposing a mouthwatering length of leg encased in shimmering black.

Devoured by lust, Daniel made a frustrated sound in his throat and turned away. 'Where do you want me to put these lights?'

'All the way round the tree.' Alfie was dancing with excitement. 'Start at the top.'

Stella handed him the end of the lights and their hands brushed.

'Did you get a shock or something, Uncle Dan?' Alfie was concerned. 'You sort of jumped.'

Putting a safe distance between himself and Stella, Daniel started winding the lights around the tree. 'I didn't get a shock.'

'But you jumped. I saw you.'

'I didn't jump.'

'But—'

Daniel sent him an exasperated look. 'Are these lights where you want them?'

Alfie stepped back a few paces, crunching a bauble underfoot. 'Oops.' He looked down guiltily. 'I've broken it.'

'I'll clean it up. Make sure Posy doesn't go near it.' Stella hurried towards the kitchen and Daniel had a feeling she'd been glad of the excuse to leave.

His instincts were confirmed when she carefully brushed up the broken pieces of bauble and then made her excuses.

'Now you've got the tree in place, I really ought to go.' Her tone was bright and cheerful, but Daniel wasn't fooled. She was finding this as difficult as he was.

'No!' Alfie was appalled by that suggestion. 'You can't go now. You promised you'd help decorate the tree. You have to stay for marshmallows and we're going to watch *The Grinch.*'

'Sounds like fun.' Stella stooped and hugged

the child and Daniel watched her pretty face soften into a smile as Alfie hugged her back.

If ever a woman was born to be a mother, it was Stella.

Which was why he'd broken it off, he reminded himself grimly. Because Stella was a woman who needed children around her and being with him would have robbed her of that chance.

'Please stay,' Alfie mumbled, his face buried in her jumper, but Stella shifted him away from her and shook her head.

'It's sweet of you to invite me but I have a million and one things to do. I'm going to be a bit busy over the next few days, but if you need anything, you can bang on my door. That tree looks fantastic. Keep up the good work. And make sure Posy doesn't go near those baubles.' Without looking at Daniel, she hurried out of the room and he heard the door slam shut.

Stella curled up in the stable, watching a Christmas movie and sipping hot chocolate, but somehow the evening didn't have any of the pleasure that it should have had.

She kept thinking of the children, decorating

the tree. Of the fun of making Christmas special for them. *Of Daniel.*

Angry with herself, she flicked through the channels, trying to find something that would hold her attention.

If she'd stayed there it just would have made things worse. It was bad enough still being in love with Daniel, without having the extra torture of playing house with him.

Finding nothing to interest her on television, she opened her laptop and accessed the internet. She'd finish her Christmas shopping. At least that would be another job done.

Checking the list she'd made earlier, she pulled her credit card out of her purse.

The great thing about internet shopping, she thought to herself as she clicked away, was that you didn't have to battle for a parking space and elbow your way through crowds.

Halfway through the evening her mother rang, full of excitement and stories about her world cruise.

As she listened, Stella felt a lump building in her throat. Her parents had been happily married for fifty years and yet her mother had managed to pick herself up after her father's sudden death and build a new life for herself. She hadn't sat at home feeling sorry for herself.

In fact, she'd sold the house, bought herself a little flat in a retirement complex and used the rest of the money to travel.

Feeling humbled by her mother's drive and determination, Stella hung up and promised herself that she was going to stop being so pathetic.

She was going to enjoy this Christmas, no matter what it took.

By the following day, Daniel was stressed, exhausted and feeling inadequate for the first time in his life.

Posy had woken five times during the night and ended up in his bed where she'd wriggled restlessly, ensuring that he had no sleep at all. At five o'clock he'd given up trying, and had left her in the bed while he went to put the kettle on.

It was dark outside as Daniel flicked on the kettle and leaned on the Aga to warm himself.

The kitchen looked as though it had taken a direct hit from a rocket launcher. There were streaks of red on the wall from Posy's artistic explorations and the remains of the previous night's pasta dinner were still stuck to the saucepan in the sink.

'Want Daddy.' Posy was standing in the doorway, her thumb in her mouth, her other hand clutching the blanket she always slept with.

Daniel glanced at his watch through eyes blurred with sleep. It was barely five-thirty. 'This is worse than being a junior doctor,' he muttered. 'Don't you ever sleep?'

'Want Daddy.' Her face crumpled and Daniel put down his coffee and crossed the kitchen. 'Honestly? So do I. But we're going to have to make do, baby girl. So what is it you normally do at this time of the morning? Draw on the walls? Throw food?' It was a wonder his brother managed to function, he thought to himself as he scooped Posy up and carried her into the sitting room.

Her curls tickled his chin and as her arms wound trustingly round his neck, Daniel tightened his grip on her protectively. 'You wouldn't be so trusting if you knew how inadequate I feel,' he murmured, nudging a pile of toys to one side with his bare foot.

How did Patrick keep the place looking so cosy?

Despite the Christmas tree dominating the beautiful living room, the barn felt cheerless and morose so early in the morning. As if the family living there had moved out.

And that was his fault, wasn't it? He had no idea how to inject sparkle into Christmas. Neither did he have any idea what to do with a three-year-old at five-thirty in the morning.

Feeling bleak, Daniel bent down and switched on the Christmas-tree lights and decided that it was an improvement. 'Enough light for atmosphere, but not enough to illuminate the mess.'

'Thirsty.' Still clinging to him, Posy cuddled the velvet comforter she carried everywhere.

Daniel looked at her blankly. 'What do you drink at this time of the morning? Not tea or coffee, I presume. Milk? Juice?'

'Juice peese.'

Daniel walked back to the kitchen, filled a beaker with juice and gave it to Posy. Glancing idly out of the window, he looked towards the stable, wondering what Stella was doing.

Then he gave a hollow laugh. Stella would be asleep, snuggled under a warm duvet, and one thing he knew for certain—she wouldn't be dreaming of him. Not unless she was having a nightmare.

Moving back to the living room, he rummaged through the pile of DVDs that Alfie had left strewn on the floor, found one with a cartoon on the cover and slid that into the player. Then he settled himself on the sofa in the darkness, with Posy half dozing on his lap.

At seven, Alfie appeared, yawning.

'Dad never lets her get up this early.' He curled up on the sofa next to Daniel, his hair ruffled and his feet bare. 'He makes her stay in her bed and play with her toys if she wakes up.'

'I'd like to know how he makes her do that,' Daniel muttered, his eyes closing again. 'Your sister is a woman who knows her own mind.' He felt exhausted. The house was a mess and he honestly had no idea how he was going to occupy two small children for one entire day, let alone four.

As if to increase his feelings of inadequacy Posy grabbed her juice and the lid flew off. Orange liquid poured over the sofa.

'Posy, no!' Daniel made an abortive grab at the

beaker and watched in horror as an orange stain settled into the fabric. 'Oh, for—'

'Don't say it,' Alfie urged. 'She'll copy you. She's like a parrot at the moment. She's more effective than my spy toys. I can plant her in a room and get an exact reply of everything that was said.'

'How am I going to get the orange out?' Daniel dabbed ineffectually at the stain while Alfie offered advice.

'She's supposed to have milk in the morning, not juice.'

'She asked for juice.'

'Dad only bought that sofa in the summer.'

'Thanks for reminding me of that, Alfie.'

'He doesn't let us bring drinks in here in case we spill them.'

'Right.' Daniel gritted his teeth. 'Anything else?'

'My pyjamas are wet.' Resigned, Alfie slid off the sofa. 'I'll go and get dressed.' His body language was so forlorn that Daniel felt a pang of guilt.

'Alfie—what do you want to do when you come back down?'

Alfie looked at him hopefully. 'Can you make pancakes?'

His confidence at rock bottom on the domestic

front, Daniel seriously doubted it, but he didn't want to disappoint Alfie any more than he already had. He could perform the most technically challenging procedures in the emergency department—surely he could make pancakes?

'I can make pancakes.'

Alfie cheered up. 'I can do the mixture if you can cook them.'

'Deal.'

But after the fifth pancake had turned to a scrambled mess in the pan, Daniel wished he'd stuck to cereal.

'It doesn't look like that when Mrs Thornton makes them. Maybe the pan isn't hot enough.' Alfie dragged a chair up to the cooker, clambered up and reached for the pan. '*Ow!* Ow, the handle was hot.' Bursting into tears, he jumped off the chair, sobbing and holding his hand.

Daniel felt a white-hot flash of panic and for a moment he couldn't think.

'Cold water,' he muttered, scooping the child up and sprinting to the tap. 'Hold it under cold water. Is it bad? How bad is it? God, I'm sorry, Alfie. That was my fault. I shouldn't have let you touch that pan.'

'It was my fault,' Alfie sobbed, trying to pull his hand away from the stream of water. 'Can we stop this now? It's so *cold.*'

'It's meant to be cold. It will help the burn,' Daniel said through gritted teeth, discovering that his own hands were shaking. 'Just hold it there a bit longer. Good boy.'

Posy started crying and Daniel felt his head pound.

This was hopeless. He just wasn't the right person for this job.

Switching off the tap, he examined Alfie's fingers. 'I think they're all right.' Relief rushed through him and he made a mental note not to let either child anywhere near the kitchen again. Somehow he had to occupy the pair of them without any more mishaps. 'Can you sit on the chair for a minute while I see to Posy?'

An hour later he was at the end of his tether and he picked up the phone and dialled Andrea's number.

She arrived an hour later, dressed in a slinky wool dress and suede boots that weren't designed for snow or outdoor life. 'I wasn't ex-pecting a lunch date today. Quite romantic.' Her eyes slid to his shoulders. 'You look good in that jumper. Macho. Sexy. But I thought you were supposed to be looking after the kids. Who's babysitting?'

'Babysitting?' Exhausted and exasperated, Daniel looked at her, wondering why he didn't feel the same rush of lust that he did when he looked at Stella. 'We're babysitting. And we're cooking lunch here. You're going to help me amuse the kids. It will be fun. We can do Christmas things.' *Whatever they were...*

Andrea gave a disbelieving laugh, as if he'd suggested she strip naked and indulge in a food fight. 'Dan, I agreed to see you today because I thought you wanted to spend some time together. I allow myself one day off a week and I don't intend to spend it sweating in front of a stove and playing Monopoly with kids who aren't even mine. You said yes to this, not me. And for the record, I don't think you should have said yes. You're too soft.'

'Those "kids" are my niece and nephew,' Daniel said thinly, 'and I said yes because my brother needed my help.'

'Why didn't he just pay someone to do it?'

'Because he wanted family.' Daniel looked at her red hair and her perfectly made-up face and tried to feel something other than disappointment. 'Would you really have said no in my position?'

'Absolutely.' Her tone was devoid of sympathy. 'You make choices in life, Daniel, and you have to live with those choices. Your brother chose to have kids. They're his problem, not yours.'

'Actually, I don't see them as a problem.'

'Really?' One sculpted eyebrow lifted. 'You don't exactly look as though you're having the time of your life.'

'Uncle Daniel, Posy's just been sick on the floor.' Alfie appeared next to him, Mary and Joseph playing around his ankles.

'I'm coming,' Daniel said gruffly, his eyes on Andrea's face. 'Spend the day. I'm not asking you to have babies, just to muck in with me for one day. We could have fun.'

'Fun is a weekend in Paris or a Michelin-starred restaurant.' One wary eye on the kittens, Andrea backed towards the door. 'Keep those things away from my suede boots. Dan, if you can get a babysitter, call me. Otherwise I'll speak to you when this is over. And next time Patrick asks you, just say no.'

'Patrick is my brother,' Daniel intercepted the kittens before they could escape through the open door. 'And I love his kids.' He just didn't love the complexities that went with the children. It made him feel hugely inadequate.

Andrea looked at him for a moment, a strange smile playing around her glossy red mouth. 'For a guy who doesn't want kids, you look pretty comfortable with those kittens in your arms. Maybe you ought to stop kidding yourself.'

Daniel watched her walk back to her shiny red sports car, waiting to feel regret. Andrea was perfect for him, wasn't she? She was intelligent, strong, and she wasn't embarrassed to admit that she didn't want children. She was just like him, in fact.

So why wasn't he running after her?

CHAPTER SEVEN

HE'D invited the lawyer over.

Telling herself that she didn't care who Daniel saw, Stella curled up in front of the wood-burning stove, sipping her second mug of coffee and staring at the mountains. The Sunday papers were strewn in front of her and she had the prospect of a lazy day doing nothing.

Despite the fact she'd had a terrible night, she should have felt relaxed and happy.

Instead, her head was full of images of Daniel and his red-haired beauty, playing with the children and having fun.

Infuriated with herself, she switched on her laptop. Another forty men had left their details and she wondered why she couldn't be more enthusiastic.

The prospect of dating anyone had lost its appeal.

Forcing herself to concentrate, she identified two that sounded interesting.

'Stella?' Alfie burst through the door, bringing snow and mud with him.

'Whoa!' Stella sprang from the sofa and caught him in her arms before his muddy boots made contact with the cream rug. 'What's the rush?' Through the open door she couldn't help noticing that the lawyer's car was gone.

Why hadn't she stayed?

Was she coming back later?

'I just wanted to see you.' Alfie's shrug was a little too casual and he clung to her more tightly than usual. 'I thought we could hang out, you know?'

Stella focused on his face, sensing that he was close to tears. 'That would be nice.' She helped him pull off his boots. 'Do you want to help me on the computer?'

'Yeah, why not? Maybe I could email Dad.'

Hearing the wobble in his voice, Stella pulled up a chair. 'Good idea. Let's do that. He'll be back very soon. How are you getting on over there?'

'It just doesn't feel like it should.' Alfie typed with one finger. 'It doesn't feel like—like Christmas.'

'Daniel bought you a wonderful tree yesterday.'

Alfie pressed 'send', staring at the screen as his email flew into cyberspace. 'The tree's great. It isn't the tree. It's everything else. I don't know.' He drooped slightly and Stella slid her arm round his shoulder.

'There's a problem?'

'There are lots of problems. Uncle Daniel just doesn't do it right.'

'But he's trying,' Stella said softly, smoothing his hair away from his face. 'He's there with you, trying his best. Isn't that what counts?'

'I suppose.' Alfie thought about that. 'I thought it would be cool being able to do what we liked, but it isn't cool. The sofa's wet, my favourite DVD is scratched and just now he trod on my remote-control car.'

Stella hugged him. 'All those things can be sorted out.'

'The worst thing is that Uncle Daniel can only do one thing at a time, so I'm not going to get any lunch because he can't take his eye off Posy. And I didn't get breakfast because the pancakes were scrambled.' Suddenly he looked very tired and very young. 'Do you think Dad will be back soon? How long can a person be without food before they starve to death? And Uncle Daniel rang the newspaper last night and advertised the kittens.' He burst into tears and Stella rocked him gently, knowing that he was just tired and disturbed by the change in his routine.

'Shh,' she soothed. 'You know you can't keep all the kittens, Alfie.'

'I wish I could keep Gabriel, too.' He wiped his face on her jumper. 'Dad's going to be so mad with me when he comes home.'

'Why is he going to be mad with you?'

'Because I've done something,' Alfie muttered, and Stella eased him away from her and looked at him.

'What have you done?'

'I'm not telling you. Then you can't be blamed. I expect Dad will blame Uncle Dan, because he was in charge.'

Stella wondered what the little boy had done and made a mental note to mention it to Daniel when she next saw him.

Then she realised that this whole situation was ridiculous. She was lonely and Daniel was struggling.

'Come on. I'm going to spend the day with you, if Daniel doesn't mind.' Stella stood up decisively, took his hand and walked to the door. 'Put your boots back on.'

'Really? You're going to spend the day?' Alfie's face lit up like the Christmas tree and Stella smiled.

'Really.'

It was pathetic, she told herself, *staying away because she couldn't cope with seeing him. Was she five or twenty-five?* 'Come on. Let's go and see if Daniel needs some help.'

'Of course he needs help.' Alfie tugged on his boots. 'That's why he rang that woman.'

'What woman?'

'The scary one with the sharp face who doesn't like animals or kids.'

The lawyer. Stella reached for her own boots. 'I saw her car.'

'Don't be upset about it. She was *useless.*' Alfie's tone was disparaging. 'She almost jumped on the chair when she saw the kittens. What a wimp. Uncle Daniel asked her to spend the day with us and she said no—which is a good thing because there was no *way* I wanted to spend my day with *her*. I want to go to the park and I bet she hates monkey bars.'

'You're hard to please, Alfie Buchannan.'

'Yes, well, Uncle Daniel was *not* impressed.'

Trying not to feel pleased about that, Stella bit her lip. 'So what's he doing at the moment?'

'When I left he was clearing up Posy's sick.'

'Seriously?'

'Why are you surprised? He's a doctor. He's used to gross stuff.' Alfie shuddered. 'Anyway, I thought if I hung out with you I might actually get to eat something when it's lunchtime. Any chance of those gingerbread men you made the other day?'

'Maybe.' Stella opened the front door and Alfie frowned at her.

'Are you sure about this? I thought you guys found it difficult being around each other?'

Stella found herself speechless. 'I—er…'

'That's why you went home yesterday, isn't it? He looks at you—you look at him. Then you go pink.' Alfie sighed. 'I may only be ten, but I'm not stupid. I have eyes. I can see he wants to kiss you. And I can see you want to kiss him. I know about sex.'

'Alfie!'

'I guess it's hard because you don't want to end up getting divorced.' He looked wise. 'I understand that. Divorce is no picnic.'

Suspecting that his parents' divorce had affected him far more deeply than anyone would imagine, Stella pulled him into her arms and hugged him tightly. 'You're a sweet boy, have I told you that lately?'

'I'm not sweet. Sweet is for babies and I'm grown up. I'm cool,' he muttered. 'So—are you going to come and cook something?'

'Stella?' Daniel's voice came from behind her, sharp with anxiety. 'Have you seen Alfie?'

'He's right here. Alfie? Didn't you tell Daniel you were coming to see me?' Stella stood to one side so that he could see the child and Daniel closed his eyes briefly, some of the colour returning to his cheeks.

'Don't do that again, Alfie,' he snapped. 'Do you have any idea how worried I've been? I've been looking everywhere for you. I thought—' He broke off and let out a long breath.

'Don't yell at me! I wanted to see Stella.' Alfie glared at him, a sheen of tears in his eyes. 'This isn't like Christmas! It doesn't even feel like home. I want Dad to come back.' His voice broke and Stella was about to intervene when Daniel dropped to his haunches and hauled the boy into his arms.

'Alfie, I'm sorry,' he muttered, holding him tightly, 'I'm really sorry. I'm sorry I shouted, but I was worried. Not that that's a decent excuse. I'm sorry I'm useless at making it like Christmas.' He released the child slightly so that he could look at him. For a moment he was silent and then he gave a sigh, as if resigning himself to talking about something he hated talking about. 'My parents didn't really do Christmas when I was young so it isn't something I'm good at. We didn't have all those routines and rituals that you do.' He pushed his fingers through Alfie's hair, a lopsided smile on his face. 'You didn't use a comb this morning.'

'Couldn't find one.'

'I'll try and find one for you.' Daniel paused for a moment, clearly choosing his words carefully. 'Why don't we go back home, make ourselves a drink and you can tell me how you'd like to spend your day.'

'I like making stuff. Cards. Paper chains.

Robins.' Alfie peeped up at him. 'It gets pretty messy. It means lots of glue and glitter and—'

'Where does your Dad let you do that?'

'On the kitchen table. Or on newspaper on the living-room floor.'

'Sounds good to me.' Daniel nodded enthusiastically. 'Do we have everything you need in the house or do we need to go shopping?'

'I can take a look and let you know.'

'Good. Let's do that.' Daniel took the boy's face in his hands, his eyes gentle. 'I'm sorry about the wet pyjamas, the scratched DVD and the broken car. And I'm *really* sorry about your hand.' He glanced up at Stella, who was standing there stunned by this side of Daniel she'd never seen before.

Daniel Buchannan humble? Apologetic?

She'd only ever seen him self-assured and confident.

'Sounds like you've had quite a morning so far.'

'You have no idea,' Daniel muttered, standing up. 'Alfie? Can we try again? And this time I'll get it right.'

'It's OK.' Alfie sniffed. 'No one's perfect.'

'Promise me that from now on if you leave

the house, you tell me where you're going.' Daniel's voice was rough and he curved his hands over the child's shoulders in a protective gesture. 'Promise?'

'I promise. As long as you promise to look where you're putting your feet.'

'It's a deal.' Daniel looked at Stella and gave a faint smile. 'I'll pay you a million pounds to come and cook some lunch for the kids. Something edible that isn't burned or stuck to the pan.'

She tried not to laugh. 'A million pounds? It's lower than my usual rate—but I expect we can come to some agreement. I was about to suggest that I come and help. I'm pretty bored on my own in the stable. It would be fun to make Christmas stuff. We can decorate the house, make some Christmas cards—'

'Food? Your job is to do some food.' Alfie tugged himself away from Daniel's grip and Stella nearly slipped on the icy surface of the yard.

'Definitely food.' She regained her balance. 'You can help me.'

'Daniel said I'm not to go in the kitchen any more.' Alfie held up his bandaged finger. 'I touched a pan. My fault.'

'No, *my* fault,' Daniel said gruffly, 'and it isn't going to happen again.'

'I'm a kid,' Alfie said patiently. 'I have accidents. You need to chill.'

'I've never felt less chilled in my life.' Daniel ran his hand over the back of his neck and gave Stella a faint smile. 'If you could take over the kitchen bit, that would probably be safer.'

'Where's Posy?'

'Asleep, I hope.' Then he caught her glance and anxiety flared in his dark eyes. 'Don't look at me like that! She's in her room with a stairgate across the door so that she can't escape when my back is turned. Are you telling me she's probably fetched a ladder and is climbing out of the window right now?'

'I'm sure she hasn't.' Stella locked the door of the stable and walked back across the yard with them, noticing that he kept Alfie's hand in his. It didn't matter that he'd made mistakes. What mattered was that he was trying. *That he cared.*

And that was a good thing, she reminded herself.

It was just that it made everything harder for her.

Making the most of Patrick's well-equipped kitchen, Stella occupied Alfie with some cooking. While he was covering himself in flour, she swiftly cleared up the mess, scrubbed the remains of burnt pancakes from the bottom of the pan, and loaded the dishwasher. When every surface was gleaming, she made gingerbread men with Alfie.

He pressed the cutter through the biscuit dough. 'Can we dip them in chocolate when they're cooked?'

'Good idea.' While he was decorating gingerbread men, Stella made a casserole for their supper and then went and examined the stain on the sofa.

'That's a loose cover. It should wash. If I do it on low, hopefully it won't shrink.'

'I'd forgotten how good you are at all this house stuff,' Daniel said gruffly, nursing his coffee in one hand while he fished through a box for glitter and glue. 'You love it, don't you?'

Stella programmed the washing machine, wondering how she was supposed to answer that. 'Well, I can't say I'm in love with the washing machine but, yes, I love the whole house-and-home thing. You know I do.' It was a reminder of why they were no longer together and Daniel was silent for a moment. She knew he was thinking of their relationship and when she glanced towards him, his eyes were fixed on her face.

For a moment they stared at each other and then Stella turned her attention back to the kitchen, determined not to read anything into the moment. She wasn't going to go there. She wasn't going to hurt herself by thinking of things she couldn't have. Neither was she going to delude herself by pretending there might be a happy ever after. She'd done that for long enough.

There would never be happy ever after with Daniel.

She was going to follow her mother's example and move on with her life.

'Can we make paper chains?' Alfie bit the head off a gingerbread man that Stella had laid out to cool. 'These are delicious.'

'Don't eat too many, you'll be sick,' Stella said absently. 'Talking of which, what's the matter with Posy?'

'I don't know.' Daniel frowned as he pulled out a pad of coloured paper. 'I think she's starting a cold. It's winter. I'll go and check on her in a minute. How long does she normally sleep, Alfie?'

'A whole film.'

'How long is a whole film?' Daniel looked at Stella. 'An hour and a half? She's had about that.'

'I'll go and look. You make the paper chains with Alfie.'

She took the stairs to Posy's pretty pink bedroom, opened the stairgate and stared down at the sleeping toddler. Her cheeks were flushed and her breathing was noisy. Frowning, Stella rested her hand against the child's forehead. 'You're burning up,' she murmured softly, removing the covers and smoothing Posy's damp curls away from her face.

She felt a flash of exasperation with life. Why did Posy have to become ill when her dad was away? Daniel was already struggling.

Careful not to wake the sleeping child, she sat down on the pretty little window seat and stared out at the snow-covered trees and the white carpet that now covered the lawn. The children's swing was covered in several inches of snow and Alfie's tractor had been abandoned under one of the apple trees.

Family life, Stella thought with a pang, wondering if she'd ever have that. It was the simple things that were so precious. The simple things that so many people took for granted. When she'd been growing up, she'd always taken for granted that she'd marry and have children. That she'd give her own children the life she'd enjoyed as a child. It was what she'd wanted. It hadn't occurred to her that she'd fall in love with a man who wouldn't want all that.

But life didn't always hand out what you wanted, did it? And she wasn't the sort of woman who would have children without a man she loved.

Old-fashioned, she thought to herself, picking up a couple of stuffed toys that were lying abandoned on the floor. She was old-fashioned. She wanted a man who loved her and she wanted to have his children.

But not any man.

She wanted Daniel. And she wanted Daniel's children.

Cross with herself, Stella put the toys into the basket along with others. It was time to be realistic. She needed to be proactive. She needed to get out there and date other men and stop comparing them to Daniel.

'How is she?' He stood in the doorway, a frown

in his eyes as he looked at the little girl. 'Her breathing is noisy.'

'She has a temperature. When she wakes up, we'll give her something.'

Daniel rubbed his fingers over his temple. 'If she's ill, she's going to want her dad.'

'She'll be fine with you.'

'No, she won't.' His jaw was tight. 'I have no idea how to comfort a sick child.'

'Daniel, you do it every day of your working life.'

'No. I sort out the medical problems. I don't know anything about the other stuff. You obviously haven't seen how many mistakes I've made today.'

Stella looked at his taut, handsome face. 'What I've seen is a man doing his best in difficult circumstances.'

'My paper chain just came unglued.'

'But you made it,' Stella said softly. 'That's what's important. And if Posy is ill, you're the man to care for her. I've seen you in the department with kids. You're good. Very reassuring.'

He ran his hand over the back of his neck. 'That's because I know what I'm doing,' he gritted, 'not because I'm any good with kids. What if Patrick comes back and both of them are traumatised?'

'Is that what happened to you?' She asked the question without thinking and immediately regretted it because his shoulders tensed and his ice-blue eyes were shuttered.

'When Posy wakes up, call me,' he said tersely. 'I don't know anything about cooking pancakes or preparing for Christmas but you're right—I do know how to examine a sick child.'

Without giving her time to reply, he turned and walked away, leaving her question hanging in the air between them.

Posy grew worse as the day progressed. She was fractious, her nose was streaming and she developed a dry, barking cough.

'Croup,' Daniel muttered as he held her on his lap along with the velvet comforter. 'Poor mite.'

Wondering how he could possibly think he was no good at comforting kids, Stella carried on helping Alfie make Christmas cards.

They were lying on the rug in the living room, everything they needed spread out in front of them.

'Just one more,' Alfie said, carefully writing a name on an envelope, 'for my teacher. Do you think she'd prefer the reindeer or the snowman?'

'Reindeer.' Stella passed him the glitter. 'Not too much— Oops…' She watched as a shower of silver covered the living-room floor.

'We could leave it there,' Alfie suggested. 'It sparkles.'

'I'll clean it up later. Don't worry. Those paper chains look nice.'

'Daniel put some in my bedroom. And we put some in Dad's room, ready for when he comes back.'

Posy started to cough again, and this time the cough was much worse.

With a frown, Daniel lifted her little pink T-shirt and looked at her chest. 'I need my stethoscope.'

Alfie sprang to his feet, sending glitter flying everywhere. 'I'll fetch it—tell me where it is.'

'In the spare room. In the black bag by the bed.'

Alfie flew out of the room and Daniel watched him go. 'He's a good kid.'

'He's fantastic.' Stella was looking at Posy. 'You're worried about her, aren't you?'

'As a doctor? No, not yet. But I'm watching

her. As a man with responsibility for his brother's kids—yes, I'm terrified.' He gave a hollow laugh. 'It's hard to be detached when you know what's at stake. And it's pretty daunting, having that much responsibility. I'm counting the hours until he's back. As long as they're both still alive, I'll consider that I've done well.'

'If I had a sick child, there's no one I'd rather trust him with. Patrick felt the same way, or he wouldn't have left them with you.'

His eyes met hers. 'Maybe that was a mistake.'

'It wasn't a mistake.' Stella looked at Posy, curled up against his chest. 'She doesn't exactly look traumatised. She couldn't be in better hands.' Thinking how much she'd like to swap places with Posy, Stella started to clear up glitter.

'I noticed that you managed to remove the stain from the sofa cushion. And the marks from the walls.' Daniel gave a tired laugh. 'You're a genius.'

Alfie hurried back with Daniel's stethoscope. 'Can you teach me how to do it?'

'Yes, but let me listen first.' Daniel slipped the stethoscope into his ears, murmured something reassuring to Posy and then listened to her chest. 'She has good air entry but she had some stridor earlier when she was upset. I think some moist air would help. I'll take her into the shower room in my bedroom. It's a fairly small room. If I turn the shower to hot, it should create some steam fairly quickly.' He caught Stella's questioning glance and gave a wry smile of understanding. 'Yes, as a doctor I know that the data shows no clinical benefit for steam. As a worried uncle, I need to do something. And at least standing in a steamy bathroom is doing something. If that doesn't work, I'll take her out into the cold air.'

'You're going to put her in the snow? Won't that give her frostbite?' Alfie contemplated that possibility with a mixture of fascination and excitement. 'I learned about frostbite in school. Your toes can go black and then they drop off.'

'Why are little boys so gruesome?' Daniel stood up, still holding Posy. 'Cold air can help reduce the inflammation in her airways. I can promise you I'm not going to put her in the snow and I can also promise you that no bits of her are going to drop off.' Rolling his eyes towards Stella, he carried Posy out of the room.

Stella tidied up the remains of the glitter and stacked Alfie's cards into a neat pile. Once or twice she glanced towards the door but there was no sign of Daniel. 'You can write your cards now,' she said absently, 'and then there's a Christmas film on TV. Why don't you curl up and watch it? I'll go and check on Posy.'

She was concerned that Daniel hadn't brought the child back downstairs. Hoping that the little girl wasn't worse, she walked up the stairs and along the wide, airy landing. The door to one of the spare rooms was ajar, and she heard the sound of the shower running as she walked inside.

The door to the bathroom was closed, but that didn't surprise her because she knew Daniel would be trying to create as much steam in the atmosphere as possible.

Wanting to help, Stella opened the door and slid inside, closing the door quickly behind her so that she didn't let the steam out.

Then she gave a gasp of shock.

Daniel was naked except for a pair of black boxer shorts, his soaked clothes in a heap on the floor. 'Don't even ask,' he warned darkly, and Stella gave a weak smile, wishing she'd knocked before she'd walked into the bathroom.

He was a study in masculinity, his shoulders wide and powerful, his stomach flat and muscular.

Telling herself that it was the steam that was turning her cheeks pink, Stella stooped and retrieved his damp clothes. Her legs were wobbly and she was suddenly horribly aware of every female part of her body. 'I'll sort these out for you.' Flustered and cross with herself, she started to retreat, but Daniel reached out and caught her arm.

'Wait—'

She stopped because she had no choice, but she didn't look at him. She *couldn't* look at him.

His fingers tightened on her arm. 'It hasn't gone away, has it?'

She didn't pretend to misunderstand him. 'No.' The only noise in the room was the hiss of the shower. 'It hasn't gone away.'

His fingers tightened on her arm. 'We're a very bad match.'

'Terrible.' Her throat felt dry. 'The worst.'

'So if we're such a bad match, why does this feel so difficult?'

'I suppose because it *is* difficult,' she mumbled. 'No one ever said that the right decision is always the easy one.'

Whether it was the intimacy of the enclosed space, his half-undressed state or the topic of conversation, Stella didn't know, but something had shifted between them. They were balancing on the narrow ledge of reason and common sense, with instinct and temptation reaching out to grab them.

And then Posy started coughing again and Daniel released Stella's arm so that he could rub the child's back. His hand was gentle and his voice soothing as he murmured soft words of re-assurance. Posy's eyes closed again but her breathing was still noisy.

Stella stood in silence, aware of how close they'd come to doing something that they'd un-doubtedly both regret.

It wasn't possible to be in the same room as him and not want him, she thought desperately, wishing she'd never volunteered to help.

'She's hot.' Making no reference to what had passed between them, Daniel put his hand on the child's forehead. 'The problem with being in this hot, steamy room is that I'm raising her tempera-ture. She's probably had enough of this. I'll dress her in a T-shirt and nappy and have her on my

lap downstairs. Remind me to be more sympathetic next time a mother brings a child with
croup into the ED.'

It was as if the moment of intimacy had never
happened and Stella knew she should be grateful
for that. The last thing either of them needed
was a rerun of their old relationship.

It was a good job they had the children to
focus on, Stella thought weakly, leaving the
bathroom and closing her eyes for a moment in
an attempt to erase the disturbing image of
Daniel almost naked. Her body still hummed
with awareness and she forced herself to think
back to Christmas two years previously, when
he'd broken off their engagement. *Forced herself
to remember the misery.*

Did she really want to put herself through
that again?

No, she didn't.

It was hard, yes. Mostly because Daniel
Buchannan was more of a man than any man she'd
ever met. Not because he was insanely handsome,
but because his qualities ran so much deeper than
the glossy dark hair and sexy blue eyes.

Gritting her teeth, Stella walked back into the

living room and sat down next to Alfie who was glued to one of the *Home Alone* films.

'Daniel scratched *The Grinch* so I can't watch that.'

'The rental shop have a machine that can fix that.' Stella sat down on the sofa next to him. 'I'll take it over there tomorrow.'

She was here to help Daniel with the children, she reminded herself. And that was what she was going to do.

Daniel lay sprawled in the chair, watching Posy as she slept in her bed.

In the room along the landing Stella was reading a bedtime story to Alfie. Her voice altered as she spoke the lines of each character and Daniel smiled. That was typical of her, turning a bedtime story into a whole dramatic experience. He could imagine Alfie, too excited by what was coming to let her stop.

It was another half an hour before she appeared in the doorway. 'Alfie's light is out. He should be all right now. Two of the kittens are asleep in his bedroom but I've decided to overlook that. Are you going to go downstairs?'

Daniel looked at Posy. Her little hand was clutching a teddy bear and her eyes were closed. She looked utterly defenceless. 'I'll stay here. In case she needs anything.'

Stella frowned. 'Daniel, you can't spend the night in the chair. You're too tall. You won't sleep and then you'll be exhausted tomorrow.'

'I'm not leaving her. She could get worse in the night.' And Patrick had entrusted them to his care.

'Do you think she will?'

'I think she might.' His voice was soft as he looked at the child. 'She isn't well, that's for sure. I checked her breathing again just before she went to sleep and she's doing all right, but if she gets any worse I'm going to take her in to the department and give her some humidified oxygen.'

'You don't think you're overreacting?'

'Maybe, but she's my responsibility and I'm not taking any chances with her.'

'Why don't I stay?' Flushing in response to his astonished glance, she continued. 'I mean, Patrick has two spare rooms. I can sleep in one of them and if Posy does get worse, you can just sort her out without having to worry about Alfie.'

Daniel wondered whether he needed to remind

her of the incident in the shower room earlier. It had been hard to distinguish what had generated the most steam—the hot water or the chemistry between them.

Was she really seriously considering spending the night?

'I'm not sure that's a good idea.'

Her eyes slid to his and he knew that her mind was in the same place as his. 'This isn't about us, Daniel. We have to get past this thing between us.'

'Any suggestions how?'

She bit her lip. 'We just ignore it. This is about the children. You might need help in the night.'

Daniel wanted to ask if she had any suggestions as to how he could ignore it. He was so aware of her—*so aroused*—that his body had reached screaming pitch.

But he could also see the sense of her staying. If Posy's condition did deteriorate, it would be helpful to have her close.

'All right. If you're sure that's all right with you.'

The connection between them was as powerful as ever. The only thing keeping them apart was a fundamental difference in what they wanted out of life. And the way he was feeling at the moment, that armour felt pretty insubstantial.

And then he had an uncomfortable memory of Stella's face two years earlier—*the devastation in her eyes when he'd told her that he'd made a mistake.*

Even though he knew he'd done the right thing and that her pain would have been a million times more agonising if he'd continued with the relationship, Daniel was in no doubt as to how much he'd hurt her.

And he had no intention of repeating his mistake.

He had to keep reminding himself of those differences.

Stella wanted all this. She wanted marriage, kids and all the chaotic ups and downs that went with it. And she deserved it.

'You must be starving,' Stella murmured. 'I'll go and make some food while you settle her down. Switch the baby alarm on and then we'll hear her if she starts coughing.'

CHAPTER EIGHT

STELLA arranged some cheeses on a plate, added some grapes and walnuts and a basket of bread fresh from the Aga. Then she picked up a bottle of red wine and two glasses and carried the lot into the living room.

The moment she walked in, she knew she'd made a mistake by staying.

Daniel had lit the fire. The lights twinkled on the Christmas tree and the room glowed with warmth, the atmosphere both intimate and festive.

Stella suddenly wished the barn had harsh overhead lighting, but Patrick had gone for ambience and the setting was uncomfortably romantic. She glanced towards Daniel, wondering if he was as aware of her as she was of him.

After his soaking in the shower he'd changed into black jeans and a comfortable checked shirt and he was now sprawled on the sofa, deleting emails with apparent disregard for the contents.

Stella watched him helplessly, feeling the relentless ache of desire, wondering why on earth she'd offered to stay and torture herself. Was she trying to make life as hard as possible? Was she trying to prove something? All she'd proved was that she was a hopeless case when it came to Daniel Buchannan.

Looking at him now, she wondered how she'd ever thought she'd be able to forget a man so unforgettable.

He was everything male, from the way his shirt clung to the hard contours of his muscular body to the dark shadow that emphasised his strong jaw.

'Is she asleep?' Trying to sound brisk and practical, Stella placed the tray down on the low coffee table. 'Poor little thing.'

'Yes. Patrick called while you were across at the stable.' Daniel reached for the bottle of wine. 'Everything is going well. I took the phone to Alfie so that he could say hello—he wasn't asleep.'

'Did you tell Patrick that Posy isn't well?'

'I told him she had a cold.' Daniel poured wine into the two glasses and passed her one. 'I didn't see the point in worrying him when there's nothing he can do. And anyway, she'll be fine. I'll check her again in a minute. Thanks for making the food. It looks delicious.'

'It isn't very exciting.' She was too physically aware of him to risk sitting next to him, so instead she sat on the floor and put some cheese on a plate for him.

'You don't have to sit on a hard floor, Stella.' His tone dry, Daniel took the plate from her. 'There's room on the sofa and I promise to behave myself.'

That wasn't the problem. The problem was her thoughts.

Playing it safe, Stella stayed on the floor. 'Did Patrick say how he was getting on? Does the job sound interesting?'

'Chicago is freezing but the hospital is very impressive. He likes the people and it looks as though the post would allow him more time with the children.' His tone was even but something about him made her look closer.

'And how do you feel about that?'

'Pleased for him.' Daniel sliced some cheese. 'He deserves a break. It's hard for him here, managing job, house and kids.'

'But you'd miss him.'

He cut a piece of cheese. Studied it. 'I'd survive.'

'Oh, for goodness' sake!' Exasperated, Stella put her wine down on the table. 'Why do you men find it so hard to express their emotions? What's wrong with admitting that you'd miss your brother if he took this job?'

Daniel was silent for a moment. 'I suppose I don't want to think about it.' He drew his hand over his face, his expression suddenly weary. 'That's my way of dealing with it. And it works for me.'

And suddenly she knew how upset he was about the prospect of his brother relocating.

'Do you think it's the right thing for him to do? It seems like a long way.'

He gave a lopsided smile. 'Maybe I'll follow his example. I'm sure they need emergency doctors in Chicago.'

Stella's heart dived and she was appalled by how sick she felt at the thought of Daniel moving to America.

They weren't together, she reminded herself furiously, so what difference did it make? In fact, it would probably be a good thing. It would force her to make the break she obviously found so hard to do herself.

On the other hand, the thought of him living so far away left a gaping hole in her insides.

'Do you have everything ready for Alfie tomorrow?' Swiftly, she changed the subject.

'His school bag is by the door. He finished his maths homework. Did I miss anything?'

Stella smiled. 'I don't think you've missed anything. You've done a great job.'

'If by that you mean that the house is still standing and the kids are alive, then I suppose you're right. We'll ignore the significant casualties along the way.' He frowned as one of the kittens jumped onto the sofa. 'At least I haven't trodden on one of those yet.'

'The kittens are so gorgeous.' Stella scooped the animal into her hands and made a fuss of it. 'Don't you think they're cute?' She placed the kitten carefully in her lap and stroked it gently. 'This is the feisty one. He was trying to attack the Christmas tree earlier. The other two are sleeping in Alfie's bed.'

Daniel yawned. 'I probably should have banned that.'

'He's happy and the kittens are happy.' She fussed over the kitten, wishing that Daniel had less of an impact on her. 'It's only another three days to go before Patrick comes back.'

'Posy won't be well enough to go to the crèche tomorrow.'

'Are you going to ask Mrs Thornton to sit with her?'

'No.' He leaned forward and put his plate down on the table. 'I've rung the hospital—pulled some strings. I'm going to take the next few days off.'

Her hand resting on the kitten's soft fur, Stella gave a disbelieving laugh. 'How did you manage that? It's the middle of winter—the department is busier than ever.'

'Ben agreed to swap with me.'

'That was kind of him. He's a nice guy. Ellie is a lucky girl.' Stella felt a stab of envy, thinking of Ellie with her gorgeous husband and her two lovely children. 'And what do you have to do in return?'

'I'm working Christmas.'

'You're working Christmas Day instead of Ben?'

'He has a family.' Daniel leaned back against the sofa and stretched out his legs. 'Christmas is important to him.'

Whereas, to Daniel, it didn't seem to matter at all. Suddenly she wanted to know. She *needed* to know. 'You really hate Christmas, don't you?'

'It isn't my favourite time of year, that's true.' An ironic smile touched his mouth. 'I'm pretty sure it isn't yours, either, after what I did to you two years ago.'

'I love Christmas,' Stella said simply. 'What happened between us didn't change that.'

Daniel's eyes glittered in the firelight. 'I'm glad I didn't ruin it for you.'

'Until I heard you talking to Alfie, I didn't realise that you found Christmas so hard.' Stella broached the subject hesitantly. 'You obviously don't have very good memories.' She knew she was touching a nerve and, for a moment, she thought he wasn't going to respond.

He stared into the fire, a blank expression in his eyes. And then he stirred. 'I don't have a single happy memory of Christmas and I'm sure that if you asked Patrick, he'd say the same thing.'

The kitten squirmed on Stella's lap and she stroked it, wanting to know more but cautious about saying the wrong thing. 'Did your parents not celebrate?'

'They didn't see being trapped in the house together over the festive season as something to celebrate. It just made the battle all the more intense,' Daniel drawled softly. 'Hand-to-hand combat instead of long-range missiles. The rest of the year my father spent as much time at work as possible. It minimised the opportunities for conflict. At Christmas, there was no opportunity for escape. They were trapped together. And we were trapped with them.' He gave a humourless laugh. 'Patrick and I used to pretend that we were prisoners of war.'

Stella thought about her own Christmases as a child. *About being wrapped in love and laughter.* Decorating the tree, playing games, the carol service in the village church, cooking with her mother…

'If they were so unhappy, why didn't they divorce?'

'The official line was that they stayed together for the sake of the children.' Daniel's voice was loaded with irony. 'But it was more for the sake of neighbours and friends. Divorce was failure.'

'And they didn't do anything to make Christmas special? No tree? No decorations?' Stella lifted the kitten against her chest, finding its warm comforting. 'No silly games of charades?'

'No. My father tried to lose himself in the television but that annoyed my mother so much she actually broke it one year.' Daniel laughed, but the sound was hard and devoid of any humour. 'I remember inviting a friend over and my mother was hysterical. Vicious. Yelling at my father. After that, I didn't invite anyone again. It was too embarrassing. To begin with I used to try and wangle invitations to other people's houses, but that was hard, too. Seeing happy families just makes you feel even more isolated when yours is a dysfunctional mess.'

'Daniel, that's so sad.' Appalled, Stella reached out to touch his arm and he turned to her with a mocking smile.

'Don't touch me, babe,' he said softly, 'not unless you're willing to go with the consequences. And we both know that isn't a good idea. I can't give you what you want.'

Stella swallowed and removed her hand. But her insides were jumping and fluttering. 'Relationships don't have to be like the one your parents had. Patrick still believes in love.'

'My brother is a fool. Carly walked out on him on Christmas Eve. The only reason those children aren't basket cases is because Patrick is a fantastic dad.'

'Yes. And you have all the qualities he has.'

Daniel lifted an eyebrow. 'Try telling that to Alfie. So far today I've burned his hand, wrecked his favourite DVD, ruined the sofa, burned his dinner and broken his favourite car.'

'You were doing your best.'

He closed his eyes, a faint smile playing around his hard mouth. 'Well, my best isn't good enough and it never will be. I haven't got what it takes to be a good father. I have no experience. I see Patrick and I think, *I'm not like that.*'

'No, you're different.' *And that was why she loved him.* 'No two fathers are the same. There isn't only one right way to be a parent.'

'Maybe not. But there are a million wrong ways and I know far more about those than I do the other.' His tone unusually cold, Daniel stood up and scooped up the tray, his body language announcing that the conversation was at an end. 'I'll take these to the kitchen. Do you want coffee or anything?'

'No, thanks. It will keep me awake.' Feeling pushed out and strangely isolated, Stella transferred the sleeping kitten to the sofa and stood up, too. 'I'll go up and check on Posy. Then I'll go to bed. An early night would do me good.'

'With any luck you won't be disturbed. Sleep well.'

They were stiff—formal—as if their conversation hadn't been deeply personal. *As if they hadn't once been lovers.*

Stella looked at his hard, handsome face and knew he was hurting. And suddenly she desperately wanted to say something that would make everything all right. She wanted to fix things. *She wanted to hug him.*

But life really wasn't that simple, was it?

The past couldn't be undone. Experiences couldn't always be forgotten. And a hug would lead to something that would complicate an already complicated situation.

Feeling tired and low, Stella picked up the small bag she'd packed. 'I'll sleep in the room with the sloping roof. Call me if you need me. Goodnight, Daniel.'

Putting the bag on the bed, she nipped across

the landing to check on Posy and found her sleeping peacefully, her breathing calm and even.

Relieved, Stella returned to her room. She had a long, lazy bath, changed into her nightdress and then slid under the duvet and switched on her laptop.

'All right, Mr handsome hunk, shall we meet up before Christmas?' Determined to push forward in her quest to meet someone else, she scrolled through the messages people had left her.

After an hour of staring at the screen and not really seeing anything that was going on, Stella gave up and closed the computer. None of them was Daniel.

And that was a good thing, wasn't it?

She'd ended their relationship because they didn't want the same thing. She didn't want or need another Daniel!

Perhaps she would go to the hospital Christmas party after all. Try and meet someone the old-fashioned way.

She heard Daniel's footsteps on the landing and froze, wondering if he'd tap on her door. *Hoping?* When the footsteps moved past, she found that she'd been holding her breath.

Exasperated with herself, she flicked off the light and slunk under the duvet. She was a sad, sad case. Maybe it would be a good thing if he did move to Chicago. Maybe that would force her to get on with her life instead of staying in this state of romantic limbo, comparing everyone to Daniel.

'How is Daniel coping?' Ellie locked the drug cupboard and slipped the keys back into her pocket. 'When is Patrick due back?'

'Tonight. And Daniel was still alive last time I looked. Just.'

'Posy's better?'

'Yes, fortunately. But Daniel didn't want her to go back into the crèche.'

Ellie gave her a curious look. 'So he's spent three days with her? I thought he was allergic to children.'

'It's not as simple as that.' Stella found it a relief to talk to someone. 'It's more that he thinks he's going to mess them up.'

'Is he good with her?'

'Oh, yes, but he can't see it. He's been painting with her. The entire house is covered in artwork.' Stella walked with her towards the reception area where the board was flashing up a waiting time of two hours. 'And this morning he was making her a papier mâché snowman because there wasn't enough snow outside to build a real one.'

'Oh…' Ellie's eyes filled with tears and she covered her mouth with her hand. 'That's so gorgeous.'

'Posy thought so. She was covered in glue and bits of newspaper and I doubt her fairy pyjamas will survive the experience, but I've never seen a child so happy.'

Ellie sighed. 'There's something about a big strong man looking after a little child that turns me to jelly. Are you the same?'

'Everything about Daniel turns me to jelly,' Stella said gloomily. 'That's the problem. It doesn't matter that he's totally wrong for me. I still want him. I'm thinking of seeing a counsellor. I need a twelve-step programme or whatever they're called.'

'You don't think that caring for the kids might have changed his mind about having them?'

'No.' Stella lifted a set of notes from the pile. 'If anything, it seems to have convinced him that he's made the right choice.'

'Why?' Ellie ducked under a bunch of mistletoe and walked into the reception area. 'It sounds as though he's done a brilliant job.'

'He doesn't think so.' With a resigned shrug, Stella waved the notes. 'I'd better get on. That road traffic accident this morning has increased the waiting time. Everyone is slipping and sliding on those pavements doing their last-minute shopping.'

'Wait just a minute.' Ellie reached into a drawer and handed her a slip of paper. 'Secret Santa.'

'What about it?'

'Everyone has to buy a present for someone. Just £5. Chocolates. Bottle of wine. Joke book. Whatever, but if that's my name on that piece of paper make sure it's chocolates.' Ellie grinned. 'We're going to put all the presents under the tree in the staffroom and have a grand opening. Which reminds me—are you going to the Christmas party? They need to know numbers by tomorrow.'

Stella hesitated. 'I don't know…'

'You must go,' Ellie urged, handing her another piece of paper. 'It's at the outdoor ice rink that they've set up by the lake. Little twinkly lights everywhere, Christmas carols and mulled wine. So romantic.'

Stella decided not to point out that she didn't have anyone to be romantic with. 'I'll think about it.' But that noncommittal remark wasn't enough for Ellie.

'Oh, *please* go. You're a fantastic skater, I remember you taking a bunch of us a few years ago. If nothing else, you have an evening out, get some exercise and impress the men with your triple salco toe loops or whatever they're called. We can have a lovely girly bonding session on the ice. There's no chance I'll catch Ben skating—you know what men are like. He'll be at the bar with the guys. I need someone to peel me off the ice.'

Stella laughed. 'I'll think about it.'

'And you're sure you don't mind working Christmas Day?'

Stella shrugged. 'It's fine.' Given the option of working or sitting in the stable on her own, she was going to choose to work, even if working meant that she'd be shoulder to shoulder with Daniel. 'Are you and Ben going away?'

'No. Family Christmas at home, everyone welcome. Which basically means disorganised chaos. We'd love you to come over after you finish here. There'll be loads to eat.'

Stella smiled, touched by Ellie's generosity. 'Thanks. But I'll probably be so tired I'll be glad to get home and be on my own.'

'Stella, you can't be on your own on Christmas Day! It's a time to be with people! If you don't sit there grinding your teeth, desperate to get away from everyone, it just doesn't feel like Christmas! And what about turkey? Crackers? Presents? Silly hats? Too much champagne?' Ellie sounded appalled and Stella managed a smile.

'If that's a description of your typical Christmas then I might come after all.'

'I hope you do.' Ellie gave Stella a quick hug and Stella felt a lump in her throat.

She had lovely friends, she reminded herself. People who cared about her.

Maybe she didn't have a family of her own, but life wasn't all about finding that one special person you wanted to be with.

But, for the first time ever, she wasn't looking forward to Christmas.

Patrick's arrival home was accompanied by a flurry of excitement and an even larger flurry of snow.

'If I'd waited twenty-four hours I wouldn't

have had to struggle with that papier mâché snowman,' Daniel observed as he sutured a laceration on a girl's leg while Stella helped. 'We could have made the real thing.'

'You still can. And I'm willing to bet that papier mâché snowman will still be in Posy's life in five years' time.' Stella gave the girl a tetanus injection. 'I'm sure she's missing you.'

'Probably in the same way Alfie is missing all the toys that I managed to damage,' Daniel drawled, tying off the final stitch and then applying a dressing. He smiled at the girl on the trolley. 'That was a dramatic end to a Christmas party. How are you getting home?'

'Is that an offer?' Still tipsy, the girl looked at him flirtatiously and Daniel gave a faint smile.

'It was a concerned question. I can see you've been drinking. Not a good end to the office party, spending an hour in here.'

'Actually, it was a great improvement on the office party. For a start, you're five times better looking than anyone I work with. And if I wasn't here, I'd still be there, which would mean dodging my hideous boss who was dressed as Santa.' The girl swung her legs over the side of the trolley and stood up shakily. 'He was going "Ho, ho, ho" and pinching all the girls' bottoms. That's why I cut my leg. I dived to one side and slipped on someone's abandoned sausage roll.'

Stella giggled. 'Sounds like a great party.'

'It's one of those parties where you know if you don't watch yourself, you're going to end up losing your job.' The girl looked down at herself gloomily. 'This outfit is ruined. I wish I hadn't drunk anything. I feel dizzy.'

Stella frowned, concerned. 'Is there someone at home for you?'

'My flatmate. I suppose I'd better call a taxi. I don't want to lose my licence on top of everything else. Thanks for stitching me up, you delicious doc.' She gave Daniel a sultry smile and scribbled her phone number on a scrap of paper. 'Any time you want to play doctors and nurses—call me.'

Daniel lifted a hand and refused the paper that she was thrusting at him. 'Thanks, but I don't want to be struck off just yet.'

The girl gave a good-natured smile and stuffed the paper into her pocket. 'Oh, well, you can't blame me for trying.' She slid her arms into her coat. 'Have a good Christmas. Whenever I watch those medical soaps on TV, I think it always looks really exciting. There's usually some sort of major accident or something, isn't there? Drama, drama, drama. Someone held at gunpoint, or a train crash.'

'That's TV. They're competing for viewers. In real life we're hoping for a really uneventful Christmas,' Stella said hastily, handing her an information sheet and urging her towards the door. 'I want to eat mince pies, not spend the day sticking people back together.'

But she had a feeling that she was going to spend Christmas Day avoiding Daniel.

Since looking after Patrick's children, everything seemed worse. Up until then Daniel had managed to convince her that he'd be a terrible father, but she knew now that it wasn't the case. He'd be a *wonderful* father. The best.

That precious time they'd spent together had given her a tantalising glimpse of a future more perfect than anything in her dreams. And that glimpse had left her impossibly sad because Daniel still didn't see it the way she did.

CHAPTER NINE

STELLA sat in the back of the taxi, having a moment of doubt.

She shouldn't have come.

It was a Christmas party, for goodness' sake, and she wasn't very good company.

She frowned crossly. Who was she kidding? The reason she didn't want to go was because Daniel was going to be there.

'Are you going to sit there all night, love?' The taxi driver was watching her in his rear-view mirror. 'What's wrong?'

'Can you take me back home again?' Stella slid down slightly in the seat, hoping that no one would see her. 'I've changed my mind.'

The taxi driver looked at her thoughtfully. 'Man trouble?'

'Sort of.' Stella didn't want to admit that she was still in love with a man who had broken off their engagement two years previously. That made her nothing more than stupid, didn't it?

'Take some advice from me—if it's a choice between sitting indoors feeling sorry for yourself or going out and meeting people, always go out.' His voice was gruff. 'I remember after my Lydia died, I didn't want to go anywhere. Didn't want to do anything. But my mates dragged me out all the time. And eventually I started to enjoy myself. And I met Beth. Life moves on, love. But it isn't going to move on if you're on your own on the sofa.'

Stella blinked. 'Well, I—'

'What's the worst that's going to happen? You're going talk to a few people and be bored. Maybe you'll slip on the ice and break something.' He shrugged as if that was a matter of no consequence. 'Either way, it's got to be a step up from sitting on the sofa feeling sorry for yourself.'

Stella laughed. 'Breaking something is a step up from watching TV?'

'You can't be lonely in hospital, and you might meet a gorgeous doctor.'

Stella didn't tell him that it was the prospect of meeting one gorgeous doctor in particular that was putting her off. 'I'll bear that in mind.' She pulled her purse out of her bag and handed him a note. 'Merry Christmas. And thanks for the advice.'

He was right, she thought to herself as she stepped out of the car onto the icy ground. A night spent alone in front of the television feeling sorry for herself was the coward's way out. All right, so it was hard not being with Daniel. But life *was* hard. She needed to get a grip.

If her mother could manage a world cruise at her age, then she could manage a hospital Christmas party.

'Stella!' Ellie slithered over to her, her hand in Ben's. 'Isn't it a perfect evening?'

Ben looked at his wife with incredulity, 'El, it's below freezing and it's starting to snow.'

'Precisely,' Ellie said happily. 'Perfect for skating. We almost don't need a rink. Come on. We're already late. If we don't get a move on, they'll have drunk all the mulled wine.'

Stella tucked her arm through Ellie's and walked under the pretty arch that had been created from fairy-lights. A few brave people were already venturing onto the rink, holding the side and moving forward gingerly to the accompaniment of raucous shouts of encouragement from the outdoor bar.

'Isn't that Alan Hardman, the anaesthetist?' Stella stared at the man wobbling on the ice and Ellie giggled.

'It *is* Alan Hardman. I thought he was far too serious to try ice skating but rumour has it that he's very much in love with Alison Waterman from Radiology and she's the one wobbling next to him like Bambi. Oh, my goodness!' Ellie dug her nails into Stella's arm as the couple lost their balance and crashed heavily. 'That *had* to hurt.'

'And I thought this was going to be a night off for us, Ben,' Daniel drawled, strolling up to them, two steaming mugs of mulled wine in his hands. 'Obviously not. Get the traction ready.'

Stella felt her heart rate double as she looked at him.

Wearing a thick jumper with black jeans, Daniel looked nothing like a respectable emergency specialist.

He handed her and Ellie a drink and then pushed his hands into the pockets of his jeans, watching the skaters with amusement. 'Which idiot thought that this was a good venue for a party? If everyone breaks a bone, there'll be no one left in the hospital to look after the patients.'

'Stella won't break anything.' Ellie curved her hands around her hot drink. 'She skated as a child and she's awesome.'

Aware of Daniel's curious glance, Stella blushed. 'I always loved dancing. Ice skating was an opportunity to release my inner ballerina.'

'Ben?' Daniel lifted an eyebrow. 'Do you fancy a spin on the ice to release your inner ballerina?'

'I think Alan Hardman is releasing his inner elephant,' Ellie observed, giggling as the anaesthetist crashed to the ice again.

Daniel winced. 'Somebody ought to drag him off before he ends the evening in our department.'

Ben grinned. 'You'll have the chance to release your inner orthopaedic surgeon.'

'Aren't you guys drinking?' Stella sipped the spiced wine and Daniel shook his head.

'If I'm going to have to deal with major trauma, I'd rather be sober. It's hard to align bones when you're seeing double.'

'I can't drink. I can't take the morning headache.' Ben adjusted Ellie's woolly hat, an affectionate look in his eyes. 'I'm on early baby duty tomorrow. It's Ellie's turn for the lie-in. That means getting up at six in the morning ready to rock and roll.'

Daniel gave a sympathetic smile. 'Until I looked after Patrick's kids, that comment wouldn't have meant anything to me. After experiencing Posy's idea of a lie-in, you have my deepest sympathies.'

Remembering the special time they'd spent together with the children, suddenly Stella felt a desperate need to get away.

They were standing here, talking, and the only thing on her mind was Daniel.

Suddenly she wished she'd argued with the taxi driver. She should have paid him double to take her home and drop the lecture.

'So this is where the action is.' Patrick strolled up to them and everyone bombarded him with questions about Chicago.

'Did you take the job?' Ellie looked anxious and he smiled at her.

'Why are you so worried? Are you pregnant again?'

Ben turned a shade paler. 'Ellie?'

'Not yet.' Ellie gave him a saucy look and Stella felt a pang of envy.

To distract herself, she spoke to Patrick. 'Did you enjoy yourself in Chicago?'

'Yes.' He took a mouthful of beer. 'Actually, I did. Thanks for holding the fort. I gather I have you to thank for the fact that my barn is still inhabitable.'

Something in his expression made her look at him more closely. 'There's something different about you,' she murmured, a frown in her eyes as she looked up at him. And then realisation dawned and she gave a little gasp. 'Patrick? Did you meet someone?'

He hesitated for a few seconds. 'No.'

'Patrick!' Excited for him, Stella drew him away from the others. 'You did, didn't you? You met someone! Tell me about it.'

'Nothing to tell.' He removed a flake of snow from her hair. 'Let's just say I enjoyed myself.'

'Is she American? Are you going to see her again?'

'I have two children and a job here.' With a rueful smile, Patrick drained his drink. 'It was good while it lasted, but not every relationship has a happy ending, as you well know.'

Stella looked towards Daniel and met his hot, intense gaze. 'Yes,' she said softly. 'I do know.

I'm sorry it didn't work out for you. You deserve to meet someone lovely.'

'Stella.' A sandy-haired paediatrician she knew vaguely walked over to her. 'Do you skate?'

'Actually, I do,' Stella said quickly, dragging her gaze away from Daniel. Maybe on the ice she'd forget. Muttering her excuses to Patrick, she handed her mulled wine to Ellie and opened the bag on her shoulder.

'Whoa—are those your own skates I see coming out of that bag?' Ben teased her, but Stella ignored him and laced her feet into the skates.

Then she removed her coat and the three men stood in stunned silence.

Ellie was the first to speak. 'Wow,' she said faintly. '*Gorgeous* skirt. And those red tights are stunning.'

'I thought they were festive.'

'You look like a very sexy helper of Father Christmas.'

The paediatrician obviously approved because he took her hand gallantly and the last thing Stella saw before he led her onto the ice were Daniel's blue eyes glinting dangerously.

He had no right to be possessive, she thought

miserably, gliding onto the ice without even thinking about it. *Just as she had no right to want him.*

Harry, the paediatrician, flailed along next to her, skating in straight lines and stopping by crashing straight into the side of the rink. Clutching the side for support, he looked helplessly at Stella. 'You've obviously done this before. Any tips?'

'The trick is not to fall over.'

'Very funny.'

Stella prised his fingers away from the side. 'You need to relax.'

He clutched her hand, wobbled and crashed to the ice taking her with him. 'Sorry. That was a bit too relaxed.'

Laughing, Stella unravelled herself and stood up, deciding that it was possible to have fun after all. And then she turned her head and her eyes clashed with Daniel's ice-cold gaze, and that single look withered her newborn happiness.

This wasn't going to work, she thought desperately. They weren't going to be able to pick up the threads of their life while they were working and living in the same community.

She was going to have to leave this little part

of England that she loved so much. She was going to have to move away from her friends— leave Patrick and the children…

That sobering thought helped her to achieve her balance and she reached out a hand and pulled Harry to his feet. 'Copy me. Watch…' Delaying the moment when she'd have to return to her friends, Stella showed him how to move, how to balance, and then took his hand and guided him across the ice.

He was slowly gaining in confidence when a dark figure glided up to them.

'My dance, I think.' Daniel stood in front of them. To the casual observer he was relaxed and confident, but Stella sensed the simmering tension in his powerful frame.

Apparently unaware of any dangerous under-currents, Harry raised his hands in a gesture of surrender. 'If you can skate into the middle of the rink with no one holding your hand, you're a better man than me, Buchannan. You win the lady's hand.'

Clearly unaware of their previous relationship, Harry gave a good-natured smile and skated carefully off the ice.

Stella was left facing Daniel.

Without speaking, he took her hand and pulled her against him, his eyes on hers as he glided backwards, taking her with him. It didn't surprise her that he was competent on the ice. Daniel was a natural athlete, physically fit and well co-ordinated. She doubted there was any sport that he wouldn't excel at if he tried.

Feeling the dangerous throb of tension, she tried to lighten the mood. 'I assume you're releasing your inner ballerina.'

'Actually, I'm releasing my inner caveman.' His sardonic smile made her heart beat faster.

'I can't see why you'd be possessive.'

'Can't you?'

All the air seemed to have been sucked out of the atmosphere and suddenly she couldn't breathe. It was no longer about skating and Christmas—it was about her and Daniel. 'Who I skate with is none of your business.' Frustrated, angry and confused, she tried to pull away from him but he held her fast. 'I can skate with who I like. I can go home with who I like.'

'Yes.' But the cold glitter in his eyes told her that her reckless remark had turned the situation from tense to dangerous. 'Is that what you wanted? To go home with him?'

'No, of course not. You know I'm not like that. And you're not making sense, Daniel.'

His hold on her didn't slacken. 'I'm just telling you how I feel. I didn't say any of it made sense.'

'In two days' time it's Christmas Eve. It's the two-year anniversary of the night you proposed to me.'

He inhaled sharply. 'I know what day it is.'

Her cheeks stung from the cold. 'And it's the second anniversary of the day you broke off our engagement.'

'I know that, too. But I still don't find it easy watching you flirt with another man.' His hand brought her into direct contact with his body and, because they were moving fast, she couldn't resist.

'I wasn't flirting, but even if I was, it's none of your business. I can flirt with who I like.' Her fingers tightened on the hard muscle of his shoulders. 'Why would you even care?'

Daniel spun her round, his mouth next to her ear. 'I care, Stella.' His voice was rough and male. 'You know I care.' He'd stopped in the centre of the rink, cleverly avoiding the rest of the revellers who were playing it safe around the edges. 'There was never any question of not caring.'

'Is that supposed to make it better? Because it doesn't.' Stella looked up at him, angry with him because it would almost have been easier if he *didn't* care. Her heart was pumping as though she'd run a race and she felt a flash of desperation because the chemistry between them was as powerful as ever. 'I care, too, you know I do. But I haven't changed, Dan. And neither have you. I don't want to spend my life as someone's girlfriend. I want to make that commitment to someone and I want them to make that commitment to me.'

Someone.

Not just someone, she thought desperately, her arms locked around his neck as they stood motionless in the centre of the ice.

Daniel. She wanted Daniel. That had never changed and it was starting to look as though it never would.

The loudspeakers were playing Christmas carols and, as snow floated silently down and covered the skaters, Stella felt his hold on her tighten.

She closed her eyes, the sexual attraction so

intense that she could hardly breathe. A stab of awareness shot through her body, spreading heat across her pelvis and making her legs tremble.

It was a feeling she'd only ever experienced with Daniel. *Wanting a man like this.*

Her desperately tempted body responded dramatically to the subtle pressure of his. She knew he was equally aroused and that knowledge heightened her own response.

'Let's get out of here,' Daniel growled, drawing her towards the side and dragging off his skates.

Stella did the same thing, her hair sliding forward in a silvery sheet as she bent to pull her feet out of the skates.

Part of her knew she ought to go back out into the middle of the ice and stay there until Daniel left, but another part of her knew that that wherever he was going to take her, she was going to follow.

Another mistake?

Without a doubt.

If she was going to be safe and sensible, she ought to rejoin a crowd of her colleagues—there was protection in numbers, wasn't there? But a reckless part of her drove her forward and she rescued her coat and bag from Ellie who was deep in conversation with one of the other nurses from the emergency department.

Ellie said nothing—simply gave her the coat and a worried look.

Without explaining himself to anyone, Daniel took her hand and led her away from the ice rink through the dark shadowy trees made ghostly by a frosting of snow and along the frozen, rutted path towards the lake. As they moved away from the noise and lights, he fished into his pocket and removed a torch.

'Prepared for every eventuality,' Stella said lightly, but her heart was bumping erratically and she was so conscious of him that every nerve ending in her body was crackling. 'I don't know why I'm coming with you.'

His hand tightened on hers. 'Sometimes it's good to do something just because it feels right. We need to talk and we can't do that with everyone watching and listening.'

Their footsteps were muffled by the snow and Stella shivered and wrapped her coat more tightly around her.

'Cold?' His arm came around her and he drew

her against him, the warmth of his body pressing through the fabric of her coat.

They continued to walk and she didn't bother asking where they were going. Their destination had no relevance. The only thing that mattered was that she was with him. And she savoured the moment.

As they reached the water's edge she heard the soft lap of the water. Behind them, in the distance, they could hear muted laughter and music but here, by the pebbled shore, they had privacy.

The intimacy of the setting stole her breath. It was just her, Daniel and the darkness.

She turned to him, intending to speak, but the words never left her lips because he scooped her face into his hands and lowered his mouth to hers. His kiss was fierce and demanding, the contrast between the cold of his fingers and the warmth of his mouth somehow increasing her excitement.

Afterwards, looking back on this moment, she decided that she'd never stood a chance.

From the moment he kissed her, the end had been inevitable because their passion had never been a half-hearted beast. What they shared had never burned itself out, diluted itself or run out of steam. His touch melted her, as it always had, and when he urged her back against the solid trunk of a tree, she didn't resist.

Excitement engulfed her and she wrapped her arms around his neck, unresisting as he closed his hands over her bottom and brought her into contact with the hard thrust of his arousal.

'Daniel…' The heavy ache in her pelvis was almost too much to bear and even while he teased her with his mouth, she wanted more. 'I want you.' Her broken admission came out as a sob. 'I know it's crazy and I know I'll regret it but I want you.' Her hand reached down and covered him and she heard the sudden change in his breathing.

It had been so long…

'I want you, too.' His hands were under her jumper and she gasped as his skilled fingers grazed the sensitive peaks of her breasts. Thick, treacly pleasure poured through her and when he threw his coat onto the ground and lowered her onto it, she didn't resist.

The ground was hard and cold through the wool of his coat, but all she was aware of was heat. The heat of his mouth. The heat of his hands. The heat of her body as the fire built. The flick of his tongue over her nipple drew a gasp from her and when he drew the hard peak into his mouth she moaned and arched against him. Sensation shot from her breast to her belly, the ache in her pelvis building and building until she could no longer stay still.

When his hand moved lower she arched her hips to help him, and when his fingers touched her intimately she dug her nails in his shoulder, feeling the hard swell of muscle through the thickness of his jumper.

The cold air licked at her exposed flesh but she didn't notice, her body devoured by the sensation created by his skilled, clever fingers.

When he shifted over her she murmured his name, the feel of him against her so intolerably exciting that she couldn't breath the air into her lungs. He was silk, velvet and steel and his initial thrust drew a shocked gasp from her that quickly turned to a moan of ecstasy.

He surged into her and erotic sensation engulfed her body. His hand slid under her bottom, lifting her, and he drove himself deep, his breathing uneven as he established a slow, sensual rhythm.

Stella stroked her hands down his back, found male flesh under the wool jumper, felt the play of muscle as he moved. Her body was a mass of screaming desire, her need for him so great that it eclipsed anything she'd ever experienced before.

'*I love you.*' She mouthed the words against his neck, a part of her still sufficiently aware to prevent herself making that admission aloud. But perhaps he felt it because he paused for a moment and looked down at her, his handsome features blurred by the darkness.

She thought he was going to say something but he didn't.

Instead, he lowered his mouth to hers and thrust deeper, shifting the angle so that the pleasure intensified to a level that bordered on painful. Without warning she smashed into a climax so intense that she couldn't breathe or make a sound.

Daniel muttered something under his breath and she was dimly aware that he was struggling to hold himself back, but he lost the fight and, as her body splintered apart, she felt Daniel's hands tighten and his mouth came down on hers.

Pleasure tore through her, thick sublime and beyond anything she'd experienced before, intensified by every movement Daniel made. Shower after shower of excitement held her trapped, but it had to end and eventually her body calmed, the madness slowly fading and leaving in its place a delicious warmth and a bitter sense of loss.

Stella gradually became aware of her surroundings—the rough ground digging through the silk lining of his coat, the cold bite of the night air and the strength of Daniel's body. She closed her eyes for a moment, knowing that she'd never forget this moment.

Regret? Later, perhaps, she'd feel regret.

Now her emotions were so confused that she couldn't untangle them. Neither did she want to. She just wanted to live for the moment.

All she knew for sure was that her belief that she could live and work alongside Daniel and still move on in her life was a delusion. She'd never move on while this man was part of her life because no other man would ever match up to him.

'I didn't use protection,' Daniel murmured, and Stella gave a painful smile because of all the issues he could have tackled that, of course, was the one that was worrying him.

He didn't want a child, did he?

He didn't want to be a father.

'It's all right.' Wondering how she could behave so normally in a situation that was so far from normal, she lifted her hand and touched his face. 'It's the wrong time of the month.'

'You're not taking the Pill?'

'I didn't have any need to,' she said quietly. 'There hasn't been any man but you.' She was still trapped underneath him, conscious of the weight of his body above hers.

'I thought you were meeting men over the internet.'

She gave a shiver as the cold licked areas of her exposed flesh. 'That didn't exactly get off the ground.'

'You're cold. I'm sorry. I don't know what I was thinking.' Daniel rolled away from her and swiftly adjusted her clothing. Then he pulled her to her feet and draped his coat around her shoulders. For some reason that she didn't understand, the protective gesture made her want to cry.

She was woman enough and romantic enough to want this to have a happy ending.

She wanted to hear 'I love you.' She wanted to hear 'I can't live without you.' But she knew that she wasn't going to hear those words from Daniel's lips.

'I'll call a taxi,' she muttered, grateful that the semi-darkness managed to help her retain her dignity. 'Is there a way back to the car park that avoids the ice rink?'

'Yes.'

'Great. Show me the way.'

'Stella—'

'I just want to go home, Daniel.' Knowing that whatever he wanted to say, it wouldn't be what she wanted to hear, Stella glanced through the trees towards the sparkling lights, wondering how she was going to face everyone in the morning.

They'd guess what had happened. And her friends were going to think she was mad.

And perhaps she was. Perhaps, later, when she lay in bed, thinking about all this, she'd reach that conclusion herself.

'If you want to go home, I'll drive you,' Daniel said gruffly, taking her hand and leading her along a path that she hadn't known existed. He opened a gate and suddenly they were back in the car park.

'I can ring for a taxi.'

'Don't be ridiculous.' He unlocked the doors of his low, sleek sports car and she slid into leather and luxury, grateful not to have to talk to anyone.

'I hope people don't think we're unsociable.' As she made polite conversation, she was painfully conscious of his strong, hard body next to hers and her own body hummed with the memory of what they'd shared.

'It's a Christmas party. Half the hospital is there.' Daniel reversed out of his parking space and the car growled its way out of the car park. 'No one is interested in us.'

He drove down the dark lanes towards Patrick's barn, his eyes fixed on the road ahead.

Stella felt numb.

Christmas Eve was just a couple of days away. The two-year anniversary of the day Daniel had proposed.

Whatever had possessed her to think she could come back here and feel all right about it all? Her love for Daniel wasn't something superficial that could be swept away like debris after a storm.

Her love for Daniel had roots. Deep roots that would always be part of her.

And it was becoming obvious to her that the only way to build a life without him was to live that life nowhere near him.

'Stella?' It was only when he spoke her name that she realised that he'd turned off the engine and that they were sitting outside the stable.

'Oh.' She grabbed her bag, her gloves and the rest of her things. 'Thanks, Daniel.' It felt as though she should say something more. It felt as though the moment was important. But she really had no idea what to say.

And he said nothing, either.

Wondering why that should disappoint her, she reached for the doorhandle.

'Wait.' His voice was a hoarse rasp and his hand closed over her leg, preventing her from leaving the car. 'Invite me in, Stella.'

The words were like the sharp edge of a knife pressed against sensitive flesh. 'I don't think that's a good idea, do you?'

For a moment he didn't respond and then he pulled his hand away. 'Maybe you're right. I'll just hurt you again, and I honestly don't want to do that. Are you going to Patrick's on Christmas Day when we finish work?' When Stella hesitated, he gave a bitter laugh. 'I guess the answer to that is "not if you're there". Am I right?'

'I'm not going to Patrick's,' she said quickly. 'I'm going to Ellie's. *You* should be at Patrick's. It's where you belong.'

Daniel rubbed his fingers over his forehead. 'I'm not feeling particularly sociable. If I ever manage to get away from the consequences of people who have drunk too much alcohol and undercooked their turkeys, I'll probably go for a walk.' Letting his hand drop, he stared through the windscreen at the swirling snow and Christmas lights that Patrick had hung from the barn. 'I might just lose myself in the mountains.'

'You should go to Patrick's,' Stella said softly. 'He's your family. He'll need you around. And the children would be disappointed if you weren't there.'

'I'll break their Christmas presents.'

'You'll make it special for them, Daniel.' And suddenly just thinking about him playing with the children was too much for her. If he'd hated kids, or shown no interest in playing with them, maybe this whole thing would have been easier.

As it was, it felt like the hardest thing she'd ever done in her life.

Even harder than the first time because then, when she'd walked away, she'd been angry with him and that anger had sustained her through the long, lonely months of isolation in London.

But that anger had burned itself out and now she just felt sad. Sad because she'd seen what sort of father he'd make.

'Goodnight, Daniel.' She slid out of the car and this time he didn't stop her.

'Goodnight.'

The exchange had a depressing finality and, as she walked the few steps to the front door of the stable Stella knew that what they'd shared hadn't been a mistake.

It had been a goodbye.

CHAPTER TEN

ON THE morning of Christmas Eve Daniel found himself sitting in Patrick's kitchen, helping Posy mix chocolate brownies.

She waved the spoon in the air. 'Lick the bowl?'

'There's nothing left to lick. At least half this mixture is stuck to your jumper, Posy Buchannan,' Daniel muttered, prising the spoon out of her hand. 'And the other half is around your mouth.'

'Are you going to tell me what happened to you at the Christmas party?' Patrick was scribbling Christmas cards on the small section of the table that wasn't covered in chocolate. 'One minute you and Stella were melting the ice, and the next you'd vanished into the forest, never to be seen again.'

Daniel ignored the sudden flash of heat that warmed his body. 'Why are you writing

Christmas cards? They're going to arrive after Christmas.'

'At least they'll arrive.' Patrick scribbled an address on an envelope. 'I was up delivering a baby all night. These people are lucky to have a card from me at all. Why are you avoiding my question?'

'Because there's nothing to say.'

'Are you going to hurt her again?'

Daniel helped Posy scrape the mixture into the tin just as Alfie shot into the room. 'I *hate* you, Uncle Daniel,' he sobbed, the breath tearing in his throat. *'I hate you!'*

'Alfie!' Patrick frowned and put down his pen. 'Don't speak like that.'

'Well, it's true.' Alfie scrubbed his hand over his face to remove the tears. 'I *do* hate him. He's made her go away.'

'Who is going away? Why is this family one big drama?' With a sigh, Patrick stood up and walked towards Alfie but Daniel was there before him.

'Alfie.' He dropped into a crouch and closed his hands over the boy's shoulders. 'Why do you hate me? What have I done?' He wanted to think that this was about the scratched DVD or the ruined remote control, but a cold premonition seeped through his body. 'Who is going away?'

'Stella.' Alfie thumped his fist into Daniel's chest. 'And it's *all* your fault. *I hate you!*'

'I guess I have the answer to my question,' Patrick muttered. 'Alfie, watch your manners.'

'Leave it,' Daniel said softly, lifting a hand to his brother. 'Alfie, what exactly did Stella say?'

'She didn't say anything. I went over there to just hang out, like we always do…' Alfie sniffed and wiped his nose on his sleeve '…and then I saw all this job stuff all over the table. And she was filling out forms. And she looked really sad. When she opened the door her eyes were all red and funny and I knew she'd been crying, but she said she was fine.'

'Then what happened?'

'She made me hot chocolate with marshmallows and cream.'

'No, I mean…' It was a struggle to keep his voice calm. 'How did you find out she was thinking of leaving? Did she say something?'

'I asked her about the job and she said she couldn't stay here and I said why not, don't you love us, and she said, yes, that was the point, she loved us too much and it was all too hard or something weird like that.' Alfie sucked in a breath. 'And I said she ought to marry you, Uncle Daniel. And then her face went all funny and she said that you didn't want to marry anyone and you don't want kids and she does.' His face crumpled. 'Why don't you want kids? Is it our fault? Were we bad? Don't you like us any more?' He started to sob and Daniel tugged the boy into his arms.

'I love you, Alfie,' he said gruffly. 'You know I do. And you weren't bad. You were fantastic.'

'So why don't you want any of your own? Don't you love Stella?'

Patrick sighed. 'OK, enough. Alfie, this stuff is complicated and it's private. It's between Stella and Daniel—you can't interfere. I know you think you understand but, believe me, you don't.'

'But she's sad and I want to help.' Alfie wriggled out of Daniel's arms. 'That's what friends do, right?'

'Yes,' Daniel said gruffly. 'That's what friends do.'

Stella was taking another job? She was leaving?

'If you loved us, you'd marry Stella so that she wouldn't have to go away and then we'd all be together.' Alfie stared at him accusingly and Patrick intervened again.

'I said enough. Alfie, you have to let Daniel and Stella sort it out by themselves.'

'But Stella is going to go away, and she loves Daniel.' Alfie stared up at Daniel accusingly. 'Why don't you want kids? Did you hate looking after us?'

'No. I didn't hate it.' Daniel ran his hand over the back of his neck. 'But it was a big responsibility and I got to hand you back after four days.' Sensing that his relationship with Alfie was going to be seriously damaged if he didn't give a proper explanation, he chose his words carefully. 'It isn't about not wanting kids, Alfie. But having kids is a huge thing. It's an important job—the most important job. If you get it wrong, you can really mess up someone's life. Do you understand?'

Alfie shook his head. 'No. I know your mum and dad always argued. And they didn't do any of the fun stuff at Christmas. Dad told me. But you're not like them. You and Stella are great. And if you have kids, it wouldn't be like that. You'd be a great dad.'

Out of his depth, Daniel looked at Patrick. 'Say something.'

'What?' Patrick folded his arms, his expression implacable. 'I happen to think that my son is talking sense. You *would* be a great dad.'

Realising that he wasn't going to get any help from his brother, Daniel let out a breath. 'I'm afraid that if I have children, I'll mess them up,' he confessed in a raw tone. 'I'm scared that I'll get it all wrong. Like I did when I looked after you and Posy.'

Alfie frowned. 'You didn't get it wrong.'

'I scratched your favourite DVD, I broke your toy car, I let Posy have juice on the sofa.' Daniel waved his hand. 'The list is endless. Do I really need to carry on?'

'That's the first I've heard about the juice,' Patrick muttered, but Daniel and Alfie ignored him.

'Kids don't care about that sort of thing.' Alfie's eyes were wide as he stared up at Daniel. 'Grown-ups don't have to be perfect. We don't need grown-ups to be perfect—we just need them to always be there and not go away. And you were there. When Posy was sick, you were there. You took time off work to watch cartoons with her and I know how boring that is because she only likes baby stuff. And when you broke things, you tried to fix them. And when it all went wrong and it was hard work, you were still here. You didn't go away when it got too much.' His voice wobbled slightly. 'Not like Mum did.'

Patrick made a sound but Alfie was looking at Daniel. 'And you *hate* cooking, but you did it anyway.'

Stunned by Alfie's passionate speech, Daniel gave a crooked smile. 'I burned your hand and I almost poisoned you.'

'Don't worry. I've bought you a cookery book for Christmas.' Alfie scuffed his foot on the floor. 'I'm sorry I shouted.'

'And I'm sorry I upset you,' Daniel said gruffly, pulling him into another hug. 'I'm sorry.'

'Are you going to fix things with Stella?'

'That's enough, Alfie.' This time Patrick did intervene. 'Daniel and Posy have been making brownies.'

Alfie walked over to the table and stuck his finger into the mixture. 'When are these going to be ready?'

'When I put them in the oven,' Daniel said

roughly, 'but don't raise your hopes. You know I'm useless at cooking. They'll come out burnt.' He felt strange. As if Alfie had taken everything inside him, thrown it into the air and it had come down in a different pattern.

His mind racing, he sank down onto the nearest chair, trying to make sense of his thoughts. *Of what Alfie had said.*

Alfie reached across the table for the rest of the chocolate bar, spreading fingerprints over Patrick's half-written cards. 'Are you OK, Uncle Dan? You look weird.'

'I feel weird,' Daniel croaked, looking at his nephew.

'You probably ate too much brownie mixture. That makes me feel weird, too. If Dad ever goes away again, you can look after me. That would be cool. What do you think, Posy?'

'Want a cuddle,' Posy mumbled, sliding off the chair and pressing her chocolaty face into Daniel's trousers.

Staring down at the tangle of golden curls, Daniel felt humbled.

The children wanted him to look after them again?

After everything he'd done—and everything he hadn't done—they still wanted him?

A lump in his throat, Daniel scooped Posy onto his lap just as the phone rang.

Patrick hunted for the receiver and answered it. 'Yes—yes, that's right. Two—a boy and a girl. They're really sweet.' He gave a thumbs-up sign to Daniel. 'No trouble at all. It doesn't matter that you're ringing on Christmas Eve. No, I don't think it's weird at all. I'll give you the address…'

When he put the phone down, he punched the air. 'Yes-s-s. Someone is interested in the kittens. She's coming round later.' He slammed his hand against his forehead. 'Can you believe I forgot to ask her name?'

Daniel just happened to be watching Alfie, otherwise he wouldn't have seen his reaction.

The little boy froze and then slid off the chair, his cheeks pink and a look of guilt in his eyes. 'I'm just going to go and squash my presents.'

Seeing that Patrick was distracted, gathering stuff together for the kittens, Daniel lowered Posy to the floor and followed Alfie into the living room.

'All right, sport, tell me the truth—what's going on?'

'Nothing.' Alfie kept his head down, dragging presents from under the tree. 'Everything's fine.'

'I lived with you for four days. That was long enough for me to know when you're lying.'

Alfie looked at him, anxiety in his eyes. 'If Dad gets really, really mad with me and throws me out, can I come and live with you? I know your flat is very flashy with lots of glass, but I promise not to touch anything.'

'Why would he get mad with you and throw you out?'

'Because I've done something.'

'I thought so.' Daniel pushed his hands into his pockets and narrowed his eyes. 'Tell me.'

'That woman on the phone…'

'The one phoning about the kittens?'

'She wasn't phoning about the kittens. Dad misunderstood.' Alfie spoke in a small voice. 'I sort of arranged something. For Dad. Only now I'm wondering if he's going to be too mad to enjoy it. If he gets really, really mad, do you think he'll take away my presents?'

Daniel grinned. 'I don't know. You still haven't told me what you've done.'

'It's bad.'

Daniel shrugged. 'As you keep telling me, no one is perfect.' And that realisation somehow made him feel light-headed. Had he been putting too much pressure on himself? Had he created this image of perfection that didn't exist? 'You'd better tell me what you've done so that I can protect you.'

And then he was going for a long walk to think about what Alfie had said.

'Why are we so busy? Christmas morning is supposed to be quiet.' Feeling numb and exhausted after another night with no sleep, Stella picked up another set of notes. 'Everyone is supposed to be at home with their families, enjoying themselves.'

'It's the "enjoying themselves" bit that's causing the problem,' Daniel drawled, checking a blood alcohol level and frowning in disbelief. 'How can anyone start drinking at eleven in the morning?'

'It's probably left over from the night before.'

'If this is left over from the night before, I'm going to be transferring the guy to the mortuary.' Daniel strode away to see the patient and Stella stared after him, wondering when to tell him that she was applying for jobs back in London.

Or maybe she shouldn't tell him at all. Maybe she should just quietly melt away.

She tried to focus on her work, smiling automatically at patients who wished her merry Christmas, trying not to let her low mood infect anyone else.

'Stella?' Towards lunchtime, the receptionist walked towards her, a pair of red antlers swaying on top of her head. 'There's a mother out there with a child who has stuck a Christmas decoration up his nose.'

'It must either be a large nose or a small Christmas decoration.' Daniel appeared from nowhere. 'Put them in one of the cubicles. I'll see the child.'

'Great, thanks. After that, we're going to gather in the staffroom and do the Secret Santa. We've got mince pies and champagne. No reason to starve ourselves just because we're working.'

'That's just what we need,' Daniel murmured to Stella. 'Drunk staff handling drunk patients. The day is getting better and better.'

She managed to smile, but part of her felt hurt that he seemed to be in such a good mood.

Clearly what they'd shared the night of the

Christmas party hadn't affected him. He hadn't been round to see her and at work he'd acted as if nothing had happened.

Which basically meant that nothing *had* happened, as far as he was concerned.

Just a bit of hot sex in the snow.

Trying not to think about it, Stella called the mother and child into the cubicle.

'Honestly, I can't believe this has happened.' The mother was pink in the face and flustered. 'I'm in the middle of cooking a turkey and I've got twelve for lunch—it's such chaos in the house, no one noticed that the bead garland on the tree had broken. My father in law almost broke his hip, sliding across the floor, and we were all fussing about him when I realised that Oliver had pushed one of the beads up his nose.'

'Dangerous things, Christmas trees.' Daniel strode back into the room and crouched down beside the little boy. 'Hello, Oliver. I'm Dan.'

The little boy looked at him. 'I've got a bead up my nose.'

'So I gather. I don't suppose this was how you planned to spend Christmas morning. Have you opened your presents yet?'

'My main one.'

Daniel pulled on a pair of gloves. 'And what was that?'

'A remote-control tyrannosaurus.'

'That sounds pretty cool. Look up for me.' Daniel adjusted the light. 'There's a chance we might be able to remove it here in the department, if it's in the right position.'

'We could always try the nose-blowing technique,' Stella suggested, and Daniel looked at Oliver.

'That's not a bad idea. Are you any good at blowing your nose?'

Oliver shook his head and his mother rolled her eyes.

'Usually he just wipes it on his sleeve. He holds the tissue, but he hasn't got the hang of the blowing part. What are the other options?'

Daniel looked at Stella. 'I could try a nasal speculum—or we could use gentle suction.'

Stella knew what he was thinking—that he didn't want to send this child down to Theatre to have it removed under general anaesthetic on Christmas Day.

'Let's not abandon the nose-blowing idea,' she

said, kneeling down in front of Oliver. 'Oliver, here's what we're going to do. You are going to keep your mouth closed and no matter what happens, you don't open it. I'm going to press on the side of your nose and you are going to blow as if you're a dragon making fire. Got that?'

'A dragon making fire.' Daniel lifted an eyebrow. 'That's a new one. What do you think, Oliver? Are you feeling dragon-like this morning?'

Oliver looked doubtful. 'I don't know.'

'Imagine that you are going to blow the biggest, hottest fire.' Stella stood up quickly and, using a tissue, pressed on the side of his nose that wasn't obstructed. 'Now, breathe in deeply and when I say go, you blow as hard as you can through your nose. OK. Go!'

Oliver blew until his face turned scarlet and the bead flew out of his nose and landed on the floor.

Daniel grinned. 'For someone who doesn't know how to blow his nose, that was pretty impressive. You no longer have any excuse for using your sleeve.'

The boy's mother breathed a sigh of relief. 'Thank you so much. I was terrified that we might actually have to stay in hospital and my husband couldn't cook a turkey if his life depended on it.' Still muttering profuse thanks, she ushered Oliver out of the room and Daniel looked at Stella.

'I didn't know that you were an expert on dragons.'

Was it her imagination or did his eyes seem bluer this morning? And his smile sexier? It was just because she knew that, in a few more weeks, she wasn't going to be seeing him again. Her brain was storing all the details. 'I don't know much about dragons,' she confessed, 'but I'm well trained in useful children's skills, like nose-blowing.'

'Yes…' He was watching her with a curious expression in his eyes. 'When it comes to handling children, you're a pretty useful person to have around.'

And that was how he saw her now, wasn't it?

As a colleague.

'Hey, you two.' The receptionist stuck her head round the door. 'Everything is set up in the coffee room. Secret Santa time.'

Secret Santa?

Stella's heart plummeted.

Oh, God, she was supposed to be cheerful and festive and all she wanted to do was slink home and hide under the duvet.

'Secret Santa. The moment we've all been waiting for.' Daniel was so good humoured that Stella felt even worse. Normally he was dour and bleak at Christmas. It was a difficult time of year for him. But today—today was different.

He seemed light-hearted.

As if everything had changed in his life.

Perhaps he'd heard that she was thinking of leaving and was relieved.

She was astonished by how much that possibility upset her.

Suddenly the challenge of looking as though she was enjoying herself seemed like too much, but she knew that if she didn't join in there would be questions. And she'd spoil other people's fun and she had no wish to do that.

Hoping that she could keep up the act long enough not to disgrace herself, Stella joined the rest of the staff in the coffee room, which was dominated by a ridiculously large tree.

Her low mood seemed to be in direct contrast to everyone else's happiness. She tried not to think about the fact that everyone else had families waiting for them at home.

She tried not to think about Daniel.

There was much laughter as presents were exchanged and Stella dutifully handed hers over to the radiographer whose name had been on the piece of paper that Ellie had handed her.

Not wanting to draw attention to herself, she helped herself to a mince pie and nibbled one side, trying to look as though she was enjoying herself. And then she glanced towards Daniel and caught him looking at her.

For a moment they just stared at each other, allowing the conversation to wash over and around them. And then finally Daniel dragged his eyes from hers and focused on the nurse who was talking to him.

As everyone lifted a glass of orange juice in a toast, Stella mumbled, 'Merry Christmas,' and the sudden stinging in the back of her throat caught her by surprise.

So this was it, then.

The end.

She'd thought she had her feelings under

control, but watching Daniel laughing with the rest of the staff was incredibly painful.

Next year he'd still be here, raising a glass with the staff.

Where would she be?

She didn't know. All she knew was that it had to be somewhere far from Daniel but the thought of that made her feel sick.

How was she going to live without him?

How was she going to get through each day if he wasn't part of her world?

She'd tried that before, hadn't she, and her life had been flat and colourless. And it was no good telling herself that she'd meet someone else one day because she knew she wouldn't. What she felt for Daniel was a once-in-a-lifetime thing. It was *real*. For her there never would be anyone else, she knew that now.

Horrified by that realisation, Stella melted out of the room and hurried down the corridor, frantically blinking back tears—refusing to let them fall. She knew that if they started to fall, they might not stop.

But holding back the tears required an almost inhuman effort because she knew that no matter how much she tried to convince herself otherwise, she never would meet anyone else. How could she? After Daniel, any man she met could only be second best. And because she wasn't willing to settle for second best, she knew that she was going to always be on her own. No family. No children.

Alone.

The corridor blurred, and Stella pushed open the door to the tiny room where they kept all the sterile packs. Shutting herself in, she leaned back against the door and drew in several deep breaths, trying to compose herself.

She'd never cried at work before. Never. It was so unprofessional of her.

And she didn't understand the awful feeling of finality that was hanging over her like a death sentence.

All right, so Daniel obviously wasn't feeling the way she was feeling, but that shouldn't matter. She'd already made up her mind that the only way to move forward was to leave and, in a way, his reaction just confirmed that her decision was the right one. She couldn't work alongside him any more.

She knew that. So why was she so upset?

The door behind her back was pushed open and she gave a little gasp and held it closed, horrified to think that someone might see her like this. 'Just a minute.' But the door kept opening and she had no choice but to step back and let whoever it was enter the room. Instinctively she rubbed her fingers over her face and smoothed her hair, trying to eradicate the evidence of her loss of control.

'Why are you hiding in a cupboard?' It was Daniel. He closed the door behind him, his eyes searching her face. 'You sprinted off before I could give you your Secret Santa.'

The fact that he'd come looking for her was horrifying.

Given her current state of emotional melt-down, he was the last person in the world she wanted to see.

He'd know it was about him.

Cringing with embarrassment, she tried to look as though nothing was wrong. *As though it was normal to take refuge in a cupboard.* 'You drew my name?' She turned to take something from one of the shelves, trying to hide her expression. 'That's a coincidence.'

'Stella, put the dressing packs down. I can't talk to you while you're clutching dressing packs.'

'Daniel, go back to the staffroom and I'll be there in a minute.'

'Actually, I don't really want to give you your Secret Santa in front of everyone.' He turned her to face him and frowned. 'You've been crying.'

Dear God, could he see that?

'I'm not crying.'

'Don't lie to me, Stella. We've never lied to each other.'

'No. We never have.' Stella focused on his shirt and decided that there was no reason not to be honest. Their whole relationship was such a mess, what was a bit more carnage? 'I made a mistake coming back, Daniel. I thought that two years was long enough for me to have moved on. I was wrong.'

'Yes. It hasn't been easy.'

'I've decided that I can't do this any more.'

His hands tightened on her shoulders. 'I feel the same way.'

'Oh.' Even though she'd already come to that conclusion herself, it still hurt to hear him say it. 'Well—in that case you'll be relieved to know that I contacted my old hospital in London and they've said that I can have my job back. I'm going to leave in the New Year.'

'Leave?' His tone was sharp, as if she'd said something surprising. 'Why would you leave?'

'Because I can't work alongside you any more! It's just too hard.' Her voice betrayed her and he muttered something under his breath and pulled her against him.

'Don't cry,' he said hoarsely. 'Please don't cry, angel. I promised myself that this Christmas I wasn't going to make you cry.'

'You haven't. It isn't you, it's me.' Her voice was muffled against his chest and she knew she ought to pull away but she couldn't bring herself to. If this was going to be the last time he held her then she wanted to make the most of it. 'I just want too much. And seeing you with Patrick's children was—it made it all worse. I'm going to leave, Daniel, then maybe both of us can get on with our lives.'

He eased her away from him gently and took her face in his hands. 'Before you say anything else, can I give you my Secret Santa?'

Stella looked up at him, depressed that he could

still be thinking about the trivia of Christmas when their relationship was ending for the final time. 'Fine,' she croaked, 'give me my Secret Santa. Thank you.' Braced for the usual box of chocolates or bottle of wine, she was surprised when he dug his hand into his pocket and pulled out a tiny parcel. She frowned. It was definitely too small for chocolates. 'What is it?'

'Open it, and you'll find out.'

'I might save it until I get home.'

'Stella, open it.'

Too emotionally drained to argue, Stella slid her finger into the wrapping and pulled out a small silver box. Still frowning, she flipped it open and stared in stunned silence at the beautiful diamond ring sparkling against a bed of midnight-blue velvet.

'Say something,' Daniel muttered, and Stella gulped back a gasp of shock.

'There's no way that cost £5.'

With a soft laugh, Daniel took the box from her numb fingers, removed the ring and took her hand. 'Will you marry me?' His own hands sure and confident, he slid the ring onto her finger and lifted her hand to his lips. 'I can't carry on like this, either. I love you, sweetheart. I want to be with you. Always.'

He was proposing?

Stella's legs shook and she felt suddenly dizzy. 'Daniel…' Then she remembered that he'd done this to her once before and the emotional trauma caused from plunging from high to low in such a short space of time was still with her. 'You— No. No, I can't. You know I can't. You gave me a ring once before. Nothing has changed.' How could she say yes after what had happened last time?

'Everything has changed. You said you thought I'd be a good father.'

'Yes, but what I didn't understand was that you don't *want* to be a father. Until we spent that time with Patrick's children, I didn't really under-stand what your childhood had been like. I couldn't understand why a man like you wouldn't want marriage and a family. But during those four days I learned a lot about you.' Her voice cracked. 'I do understand and I ache for you and I'm angry with your parents for being so selfish and putting their own feelings before yours, and for not having any idea of the impact their behaviour had on you.'

'I don't want to talk about my parents. Stella, I'm asking you to marry me.'

'I know you are.' Stella pulled away from him and forced herself to do the hardest thing she'd ever done in her life. Refusing him. *Removing his ring from her finger.* 'And this time I'm saying no. Which is what I should have said the first time. I won't marry you. I *know* you, Daniel. I know what you want and what you don't want. And you don't want this.'

'You love me.'

'Oh, yes.' She smiled through her tears, no longer trying to hold them back. 'I do love you. And I believe that you love me, but that isn't a good enough reason for you to do something you don't want to do. That just leads to resentment. I'm not one of those women who just think, He'll be fine once he's married and he'll fall in love with a child if we have one. What if you don't, Daniel? What if all you feel is resentment? Resentment isn't a good foundation for a marriage.'

'Stella, look at me.' His voice hoarse, Daniel reached out a hand and caught her chin, turning her face to his. 'Look at me and listen. You say that looking after Patrick's children taught you something about me. Well, looking after those children taught me something about myself, too. It wasn't that I didn't want children—it was just that I was terrified of failing them. Of getting it wrong. Of messing them up.'

'Daniel, I know that. I—'

'Let me finish.' His hands cupped her face, his eyes holding hers. 'I won't blame you if you won't take a chance on me again, but at least let me tell you what I'm thinking. This time it's different, Stella. When I proposed to you two years ago, I was in love with you. I wanted you. I thought I could get over my phobia about marriage and children—and then Patrick's wife walked out. At Christmas, leaving a trail of emotional devastation behind her. Up until that point I'd always believed it would have been better if my parents had just divorced. And then I realised that staying and going can be equally agonising for the children.' His tone was suddenly harsh. 'And I thought to myself, *I never want to hurt a child like that.* I won't do it. And that's why I broke it off. Not because I didn't love you, but because I wasn't sure I could be the man you wanted me to be. I didn't think I could give you what you wanted.'

'I know that too, and—'

'I was terrified by the responsibility of parenting. I suppose in my head I'd spun this image of a perfect happy family. I was afraid I could never match that image.'

'I don't suppose anyone does.'

'No. But then I realised that plenty of people get it right, even when circumstances aren't perfect. Even though he's single, Patrick is a wonderful father. Alfie and Posy are happy and confident. And someone told me recently that a good parent doesn't have to be perfect.' He gave a crooked smile. 'They told me that DVDs can get scratched and toys can be broken, and a family can still work. None of those things mess a child up. A perfect family is a family that loves each other and is always there for each other.'

Stella swallowed. 'Who told you that?'

'Alfie. And he's something of an expert.' Daniel's voice was suddenly soft and his gaze was disturbingly intense. 'He also told me that what children really need is to be loved and to know that they're loved. And our children are going to know that, Stella.'

Their children?

Stella felt the lump in her throat return. 'Daniel, we really can't—'

'We can. We can, Stella.' He lowered his mouth to hers and kissed her gently. 'I know I'm asking a lot. You're standing there thinking, It's Christmas Day and he's going to break my heart a second time. But I promise you that this time you're wrong. Make a family with me, Stella. If you're there, I know we'll do it right.'

He sounded so sincere that Stella had to rein in the urge to just yell, *Yes, yes, yes!* 'You want a family?'

'That's what I'm telling you.'

'You really want to marry me?'

Daniel lifted her hand so that the diamond twinkled under the lights. 'You think this is a joke?'

Despite the tears misting her eyes, Stella smiled. 'I think it's a really nice ring for £5. What would have happened if you hadn't picked out my name in the Secret Santa?'

'I didn't pick your name. I had to persuade Ellie to fix it for me.'

'You're shameless.' But she was smiling through her tears and suddenly Christmas was starting to feel the way it was supposed to feel.

'I can't believe you've changed your mind. I never thought that was going to happen. I'd given up hoping.'

'But Christmas is a time for hope, and I wanted Christmas to be perfect for you this year,' Daniel said softly. 'And perfect for me. Are you going to make it perfect, angel? Are you going to give me another chance? Say yes.'

Yes.

Did she dare?

Feeling suddenly light-headed, Stella glanced around her. 'Talking of situations not being perfect, I'm intrigued as to what motivated your decision to propose to me in a cupboard?' She felt ridiculously happy and if there'd been more room, she would have danced around the dressing packs.

'You were the one who chose the cupboard,' Daniel drawled, a gleam of humour in his blue eyes. 'I just wanted an intimate conversation without an audience. I thoroughly approve of teamwork in the emergency department but this is one situation in which I don't need anyone's help.' He pulled her hard against him. 'I'm still waiting for your answer. But if you say no, I have to warn you that I'm not going to listen.'

There was a sudden banging on the door and one of the nurses called out 'Daniel? Are you in there? Ambulance Control just called. They're bringing in a Santa who fell off his sleigh. Possible Colles' fracture. They think he's been drinking.'

Daniel rolled his eyes. 'Don't any fantasies remain intact? Santa drinking in charge of a sleigh? Unbelievable,' he breathed, and then he tilted Stella's face to his. 'You'd better decide quickly before we have a department full of elves and reindeer. Your answer?'

Stella smiled, tears blurring her vision. 'Yes,' she whispered. 'My answer is yes. Of course. I love you. I always have. I always will. You're the only man I've ever wanted.'

Daniel lowered his head to hers, everything he felt for her communicated in that one devastating kiss.

'Thank you,' he murmured against her mouth. 'Thank you for trusting me. Thank you for saying yes a second time. I promise I won't let you down.'

The thumping on the door interrupted them. 'Daniel?'

Daniel lifted his head reluctantly. 'We'd better go and see Santa,' he drawled, his arm still around her waist as he reached for the doorhandle. 'When we've finished patching him up, you can tell him what you want for Christmas.'

'I already have everything I want for Christmas.' Stella slid her arms round his neck, her happiness so great she just wanted to smile and smile. 'I have you. And you're the only present I've ever wanted.'